If at First You Don't Succeed, Fly Again

THE TRAVEL MISHAPS OF CAITY SHAW BOOK 7

ELIZA WATSON

ISBN-13: 978-1-950786-16-9 (ebook)

ISBN-13: 978-1-950786-17-6 (paperback)

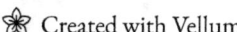 Created with Vellum

Books by Eliza Watson

Nonfiction

Genealogy Tips & Quips

Fiction

A Mags and Biddy Genealogy Mystery Series

How to Fake an Irish Wake (Book 1)

How to Snare a Dodgy Heir (Book 2)

How to Handle an Ancestry Scandal (Book 3)

How to Spot a Murder Plot (Book 4)

How to Trace a Cold Case (Book 5)

How to Pursue a DNA Clue (Book 6)

The Travel Mishaps of Caity Shaw Series

Flying by the Seat of My Knickers (Book 1)

Up the Seine Without a Paddle (Book 2)

My Christmas Goose Is Almost Cooked (Book 3)

My Wanderlust Bites the Dust (Book 4)

Live to Fly Another Day (Book 5)

When in Doubt Don't Chicken Out (Book 6)

If at First You Don't Succeed, Fly Again (Book 7)

For additional books by Eliza Watson, visit
www.elizawatson.com.

My Coffey Family Tree
Cheat Sheet

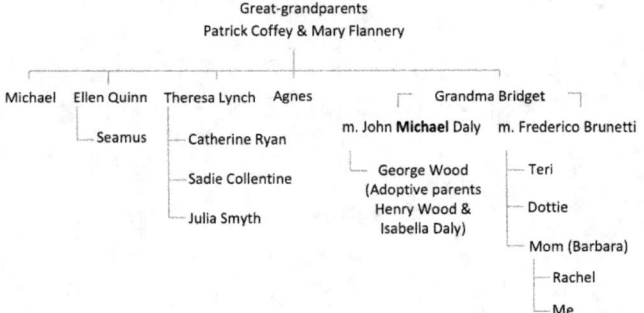

Great-grandparents
Patrick Coffey & Mary Flannery

Michael   Ellen Quinn   Theresa Lynch   Agnes   Grandma Bridget

             └─ Seamus   ├─ Catherine Ryan   m. John **Michael** Daly   m. Frederico Brunetti

                              ├─ Sadie Collentine   └─ George Wood   ├─ Teri
                                                             (Adoptive parents
                              └─ Julia Smyth   Henry Wood &   ├─ Dottie
                                                             Isabella Daly)
                                                                                  └─ Mom (Barbara)

                                                                                     ├─ Rachel

                                                                                     └─ Me

One

"I QUIT!" The young waiter slammed the stately home's large wooden door, the echo vibrating through the room and my chest. I expected the yellow-and-red stained-glass window at the top of the staircase to shatter.

Gerry Coffey's desperate gaze darted to me from across the salon. The ruggedly handsome dark-haired guy glanced between me and the door. He shifted his weight to his front foot, preparing to bolt from the Daly estate.

I gave my head a discreet shake. If he quit, I couldn't! My breathing quickened.

Car tires spit gravel into the evening air outside. The sound of freedom.

My sister, Rachel, tossed her arms up in frustration. "Where do we have to go to find reliable help?"

Gerry's broad shoulders relaxed. He shrugged off his blue wool blazer, revealing a white dress shirt rather than his usual *Coffey's Dublin* green T-shirt. His loyalty to his girlfriend, my sister, won out in the end.

I wasn't quite as loyal at the moment.

Annoyance flashed in Fanny's soft blue eyes, which matched the faint blue tint in her gray hair. My uncle George Wood—a short gray-haired man—placed a calming hand on his new wife's petite shoulder. He fought back a sneeze, then caught the next one with a hanky from his tan slacks.

"You'll have to hire from outside of England," I told Rachel matter of factly.

My sister had the nerve to look offended. She'd alienated every waiter within a fifty-mile radius of our elderly uncle's stately home in Dalwade, Lancashire. She'd done so in less than six weeks following the estate's appearance on the popular TV show *Sunnyvale*. Rachel had capitalized on the publicity, hoping to dig George's place out of debt. There were three sold-out afternoon teas daily—which started in the morning—and dozens of weddings booked into next year. The estate was closed Mondays, which we all spent recuperating.

Rachel squared her shoulders. "As if it's *my* fault these people oversell themselves on their résumés then can't perform up to my expectations."

I'd embellished my résumé during my brief stint as an event planner and had somehow lived up to my supposed qualifications. Sort of. My new fiancé, Declan, always said fake it till you make it. Something I was still doing in my quest to become a genealogist. Genealogy was my real passion.

"Nobody could perform up to your expectations," I said. "That's why we've lost three waitstaff in under a month. Before long, no one is going to want to work here. At least *one* of those event planners you interviewed had to be qualified." I had my own wedding to plan!

I'd only seen Declan five days in the past month. I peered down at my traditional Irish Claddagh wedding ring—two silver hands clasping a crowned heart with an emerald in the center. The tension in my body eased.

George let out a tired moan. Fanny placed a comforting hand on his arm. The couple's honeymoon had ended before it began.

Rachel stormed out. Her shoulder-length brown hair bounced against her shoulders, and her square-heeled shoes hammered against the wood floor.

A collective sigh of relief filled the room.

"I don't believe I've even been to the loo today." Fanny brushed a finger over the tea stains on the front of her blue chiffon dress. "And I won't eat another one of my bloody scones for as long as I live." Her gauze-wrapped forearm had burn marks from frantically slipping trays of her famous lemon poppy seed and blueberry scones in and out of the massive cast-iron oven beginning at 4:00 a.m. daily. Besides providing scones for tea events, Fanny had sold hundreds of packaged mixes in local shops, thanks to *Sunnyvale*'s actress having raved about her delicious baked goods.

I agreed with Fanny. I'd prefer not to see another scone or cucumber finger sandwich for the rest of my life after living on them for the past six weeks.

"I'm selling my home." Fanny gave a definitive nod. "Will fund the estate and put an end to this craziness."

George looked aghast. "You'll do no such thing. What about your sister?"

"I'll evict her. About time she learned to stand on her own." A mortified gasp caught in Fanny's throat. Her sister had been confined to a wheelchair for years. "I can't believe I just said that. Please don't tell her I said that. What kind of a monster am I turning into?"

"We're all just in need of a good night's sleep, dear. And a good scotch...or two." George turned from his wife and coughed into his hanky. He eased down onto a red uphol-stered antique chair that had replaced Fanny's blue wingback for the filming. His breathing quickened, a faint whistling sound escaping from between his thin lips.

"And poor George here is going to be back in the hospital with pneumonia, he's so run down." Fanny placed a loving hand on his back as he coughed.

This past spring, Declan and I had rushed from Ireland to England to find George deathly ill and in the hospital, his home nearly void of furnishings. Not having the funds to maintain the estate, he'd been planning to sell it. We came to his rescue and organized murder mystery events to save his family home. We now had enough money for a new roof, yet a roofer wasn't available for two months. In the meantime, we prayed the water-damaged ceilings upstairs didn't cave in.

Gerry glared at the door through which Rachel had made her dramatic exit. "She's about to lose more than a waiter." He raked a frustrated hand through his dark hair. "How am I supposed to quit now that you're down another lad? I've never seen this side of her, and I don't be liking it. Not one wee bit."

"Please stay one more day." So I wouldn't have to. "Things are about to change." I glanced at the clock on the fireplace mantel. "Very soon." If anyone could get Rachel back on track, it was my surprise guest.

Time to regroup. I blew a clump of auburn hair from my eyes. Without the aid of a mirror, I tossed the stray hairs back up in the clip. I swiped magenta gloss over my lips and wiped away the black mascara smudges that were likely under my eyes.

"How about a drink?" I said.

Gerry poured four glasses of scotch, and we dropped onto the red velvet chairs and couches. Fanny slipped off her proper heels and curled her nylon-stockinged toes into the rug. George glared at the photo of the show's wedding couple that hung over the fireplace—rather than his and Fanny's. Gerry undid the top buttons on his shirt and slammed half his drink. I set my glass on an ornate end table (which had replaced the flying monkey table for the filming). I missed the hideous monkey table that my dog, Mac, barked at whenever he encountered it.

Fighting back tears of exhaustion, I peered through a watery haze at Declan's reproductions of the estate's stolen artwork, which hung on the faded red walls. My favorite had appeared on the television episode—a woman seated at a library desk writing a letter, sun shining through a window. Declan was at home reproducing the painting like a madman to keep up with sales, while I was "temporarily" managing the afternoon tea events so Rachel could plan weddings. It wasn't like I could pop home for dinner one night to see him. It took eight hours to travel from the estate to our home in Ireland, between driving three hours to the port in Wales, taking a ferry across the Irish Sea to Dublin, then navigating the narrow, rough country roads.

I needed a full-time genealogy job ASAP!

I choked down a gulp of scotch, setting my throat on fire. Rather than enjoying my typical glass of wine, lately I'd been reaching for the smokey-scented liquor. My first glass had been the day a *Sunnyvale* fan had tripped down the open staircase while taking a selfie—the very staircase where the actress had made her long-awaited entrance at the wedding. That started nightmares of me stepping on my wedding dress and tumbling down the stairs. No way was I walking down that staircase, despite Fanny and George's wish to start a family wedding tradition at the estate.

Rachel marched back into the room.

Everyone tensed.

She shook jagged pieces of china from a broken teacup in her hand. "More evidence why that waiter should have been fired. Just found this—"

"For the love of God." Fanny tossed her arms up in the air.

I snapped back in my seat, surprised at sweet Fanny's outburst.

"Those mismatched china cups and saucers cost a pound each from the antique shop in town. We can afford to lose fifty of those teacups before we can afford to lose another waiter!" Fanny's shoulders trembled.

George slipped an arm around her. "Relax, dear. It'll be fine."

Rachel's bottom lip quivered, and a tear trailed down her cheek. She flinched, pressing a hand against her right side. She'd had a major kidney infection in college, and when over-stressed, her right kidney throbbed.

Gerry rushed to her. "You all right, luv? Need to be going to the A and E, do ya?"

Rachel shook her head.

"Oh, I'm sorry, dear." A tear slipped down Franny's cheek too. "I'm a complete wreck. Not myself at all."

The doorbell rang.

That was about to change.

I raced toward the entryway, a mix of relief and anxiety fluttering in my chest. I threw open the door. Instead of heels and her usual formfitting clothes, Gretchen had on black cotton yoga pants, an oversized gray hoodie, and tennies. Her long blond hair, with dark roots, was tossed up in a lopsided ponytail. Without her signature jade-colored eye shadow and black winged liner, her greens eyes looked softer, less intimidating.

"Gretchen?" Rachel's surprised reaction was better than what I'd feared.

I embraced the woman in our first-ever hug. "I'm so happy to see you."

A year ago I'd never dreamed of being excited to see Gretchen. We'd met on my first meeting in Dublin. Rachel, a corporate event planner at the time, thought her star contractor could do no wrong even when I proved Gretchen *could*, defending myself when she tried to use me as a scapegoat. Gretchen had spent the entire meeting making me feel incompetent, causing Rachel to question my abilities—at a time when I was trying to gain my sister's respect and rebuild our relationship. Also, Gretchen had once slept with Declan.

Our antagonistic relationship had taken a turn six months ago in Prague, when we'd bonded over our shared dislike for a batshit-crazy meeting planner. Gretchen had helped me capture a macaron thief and clear my name, and I'd assisted her with genealogy research. She'd even provided a testimonial for my website.

A nervous smile twitched the corners of Gretchen's

mouth. She hitched a brown designer carry-on bag up on her shoulder and wheeled a matching suitcase in behind her.

"What are you doing here?" Rachel asked.

"She's my replacement."

"*Your* replacement, is she?" Gerry glared at me after my pleading look had convinced him to stay.

"I can't believe you hired her without consulting me." Rachel turned to Gretchen. "Not that it isn't good to see you."

"She's the only planner who could meet your expectations, and whether you agree or not, we need another experienced planner. I'm only temporary, remember? My genealogy course in Dublin starts in two weeks."

The ten-week course provided a certificate in Irish records that would look awesome on my pathetic résumé. Enrolling in an in-person program assured I'd be in Ireland and not here squeezing in virtual classes between afternoon teas.

"Gretchen was Rachel's wingman when she worked at Brecker Brewery," I explained to everyone. "She's the best contractor in the business."

Gretchen looked surprised by my praise.

"We can't afford a full-time planner yet," Rachel said.

I nodded. "Yes, we can. Besides, she wants some time off the road. She's working temporarily in exchange for room and board."

"My yes, all the scones you can eat." Fanny smiled brightly. "Would you fancy butter or clotted cream with homemade jam?"

"Yes, yes, do come in, dear. Please, have a seat." George patted the back of the couch.

Gerry poured a scotch. "Fancy a drink, would ya?"

Fanny's face lit with excitement. "Oh, we could open that bottle of champagne we've been saving from the wedding."

Rachel stood there dumbfounded.

"George and Fanny can take over my role as tour guide," I said. "Which is what they should be doing. They can't be on their feet all day baking scones, making finger sandwiches, and doing dishes because we keep losing staff. They can still bake the scones, but I've hired a caterer to provide the sandwiches, and also a dishwasher."

"A caterer?" Rachel said. "We already pay a baker for the macarons and sweets."

"Maybe if you apologize to my friend Emma, she'd agree to continue making her exquisite cucumber and salmon sandwiches," Fanny snapped. "And you may soon be paying the baker to make my scones." Fanny gave Rachel a sympathetic smile. "Sorry, dear. I can't keep up like this."

The gentle woman's assertive attitude nearly had Rachel in tears again, but she nodded.

"I'll share my secret recipe with Cousin Enid if I have to."

A collective gasp filled the room. Fanny hadn't shared her secret recipe with anyone, certainly not our nasty cousin Enid.

"The staff needs to be taking proper breaks and have two days off a week," I said. "Mondays and Tuesdays starting next week. In addition, we can consolidate the teas already booked to two daily. Gerry and I can walk Gretchen through everything if he's willing to stay so I can take off a few days to go see my fiancé." I'd sent Gretchen the estate's events calendar and the afternoon tea specs so she could hit the ground running. If anyone could get Rachel back in line, it was Gretchen.

"Oh, congratulations." Gretchen gave me a sincere smile, admiring the ring on my finger.

I smiled my thank-you.

Rachel's gaze shot to Gerry. "You were going to leave?"

Gerry nodded. "Sorry. It was either leave the estate or leave *you*. Been a bloody nightmare, ya have."

My sister wore a wounded expression.

Gerry slipped his arms around her waist and kissed her. "Sorry, luv, but ya have."

"I'll be back in a few days," I said. "Declan and I've been engaged nearly six weeks, and we've barely seen each other six days." I couldn't leave poor George and Fanny high and dry until additional staff was in place. Thomas—the gardener and George's best friend—had bolted the first chance he had two weeks ago. He was designing a garden for a stately home in Yorkshire.

Gretchen looked shocked over my take-charge attitude. We'd met shortly after my ex-boyfriend, Andy, had destroyed my self-confidence and ability to stand up for myself. Being dressed in a sausage costume at the time hadn't done wonders for my low self-esteem either.

"I was only trying to get the estate back on its feet and take advantage of the hype from the *Sunnyvale* episode," Rachel said. "Strike while the iron is hot and before the couple end up divorced and people no longer want to book weddings here."

We'd all been worried that the show might have filmed two endings and the couple wouldn't get married at the estate. The home's appearance in the final episode had been critical to the estate's upkeep.

"I get it." I gave my sister an understanding smile. "But right now the best thing for the estate is for you to go to bed and get some rest before you lose a kidney."

Rachel opened her mouth to argue.

"Go!" Gretchen and I commanded, pointing to the staircase.

We exchanged surprised glances that we were in sync.

Even though Gretchen and I'd left Prague on friendly terms, I never imagined I'd one day be offering her a job. She'd once wanted me *out* of a job. Fingers crossed she'd last longer than the waiters had.

Two

THE FOLLOWING MORNING, I crept down the creaky staircase, not wanting to wake anyone up at four o'clock on their one day off. Soon they'd be able to sleep in two days. I fought the urge to sprint out the door, hop in the car, and hear the tires spitting up gravel as I escaped down the driveway. Instead, I padded across the salon's wooden floor in my tennies, lugging my suitcase so the wheels wouldn't echo through the house.

A crackling fire in the faintly lit library stopped me in my tracks. I prayed it wasn't Rachel. A confrontation at this hour was the last thing I needed. I peeked into the oak-paneled library, where Gretchen sat on a blue velvet couch, wrapped in a white velour robe, her legs curled beneath her. A teacup cradled in her hands, she glanced over from the fireplace and smiled good morning. I left my suitcase at the door, making it easier to navigate around an eclectic array of couches, love seats, and chairs, which provided seating for fifty attendees at the tea events.

I smiled at her luxurious hotel-logoed robe, *La Haute*

Boheme. "Nice robe." I had one just like it from the Prague hotel, where a kind banquet captain, Nigel, had surprised me with the gift after I'd endured a horrible workday.

"I was just there last month. Wasn't the same without Nigel. He retired. Moved back to England to care for a sick aunt."

"His aunt here in Lancashire?"

She shrugged. "Not sure."

Excitement zipped through me. "If he's in the area, maybe he'd be interested in getting out of the house a few days a week. A part-time banquet job."

Nigel was the best banquet captain I'd ever worked with. Actually, he was the only one I'd ever worked with. However, if Gretchen thought he was stellar, he was. Gretchen had been a bit intense for Nigel. His opinion of her changed when she showed interest in his quest to uncover the identity of his biological grandfather. Gretchen's curiosity about her own family history gave them a personal connection. Perhaps he'd be willing to work with her once again.

"I'll have to reach out to him. Maybe Mindy would be able to help for a few weeks during the crunch. But she's usually booked months out." I gave Gretchen a curious look. "Like you."

"I confess—I cleared my schedule when you reached out to me. Left a Portugal meeting a few days early."

My eyes widened in shock, unable to imagine Gretchen ditching a client in the middle of a meeting. I was relying on her strong work ethic to keep her from ditching us.

A sly smile curled Gretchen's lips. "I bet Oscar is still looking for a job."

I laughed, recalling how she and I'd worked together to

capture the waiter who'd stolen the macarons. "Don't think he'd care to work with us again after you blocked him like a defensive lineman, preventing his escape."

"And fell on my butt. If he hadn't stumbled backward so you could grab hold of the bottom of his suit jacket, he might have gotten away."

We laughed at the scene straight out of a cheesy whodunit. Gretchen placed a hushing finger to her lips, then cupped a hand over her mouth, stifling laughter.

"We proved my innocence," I said.

"Thanks again for asking me here to help out. It was time for a change. I envy you following your passion and knowing what you want to do in life. All I know is I don't want to do corporate events. My coworker friend is only thirty-four years old and had a massive stroke from the stress."

"Oh wow. I hope she's okay."

"She'll have a long road to recovery."

"I'm worried about Rachel losing a kidney or having a stroke. After she left Brecker, she was much more laid back. Then the episode aired, and she went into manic planner mode."

"I'll help her get a grip. I owe you one. Thanks to you, I'm getting my EU passport this month."

I'd located Gretchen's grandfather's birth record in Hungary rather than Germany, where he was supposedly born. This discovery enabled her to obtain citizenship through her Hungarian grandfather, whereas Germany only permitted citizenship through parents. Hungary was part of the EU, which would allow Gretchen to one day buy her mountain cottage in Bavaria.

"It might have been years before I discovered I was

eligible for Irish citizenship through my grandma if you hadn't told me. I might be working a meeting in Detroit right now rather than heading home to Ireland to be with Declan and Mac." I cringed. "I guess we both helped each other."

Next thing I knew, Gretchen and I would be shopping for swimsuits together for our girls' weekend in Lanzarote.

Having Gretchen in place lessened my guilt over deserting the others. During the ferry ride, I shot emails off to Nigel and Mindy, asking if they might be looking for work at a lovely English estate that had been featured in *Sunnyvale*. Being English, Nigel was likely a fan of the soap opera but, like George, wouldn't admit it.

I'd debunked the myth that his unknown grandfather was a blue blood—he'd been a convict sent off to Australia. Nigel had been glad to learn the truth and wouldn't hold it against me. Perhaps, like Gretchen, he'd feel he owed me one, even though he didn't.

Mindy and I had also bonded in Prague. While delivering a gift to a suite, I'd tried on the VIP's spa slippers to relieve my tired feet and dozed off from exhaustion. Mindy had discovered me in the room and promised not to tell. She confided in me that once on an awful program, she'd slammed a glass of scotch from a four-hundred-dollar bottle of liquor she'd delivered to a suite the previous night. Combat pay.

The 9:00 a.m. ferry out of Wales put me into Dublin at noon. No tractors, sheep, or other obstacles on the road to slow me down, I made it from the Dublin port to home in an hour despite driving cautiously. Declan's sister, and my friend, Zoe had loaned me her car while she and her sheep-herder boyfriend were on holiday in Portugal. I rounded the bend on the narrow road, and the Coffey cottage's rusted metal roof peeked over the top of the tall hedges bordering the road. I drove through the open green iron gate and admired the yellow and red flowers along the front of the small stone cottage with a freshly painted red door. The door had matched the gate until we decided too much green blended in with Ireland's landscape.

The cottage had been abandoned for decades, until Henny Penny—a pregnant hen from up the road—had taken up residence a few months ago. One day she and her chicks were gone, back to her former home. Our white rabbit, Stew, was still hopping around the yard and the surrounding fields. I continued up the drive to our Georgian-style house, once the home of Michael Daly, Grandma Coffey Brunetti's first husband and Uncle George's biological father. Michael's father was an English landlord, leasing his land to my Coffeys. Thankfully, Michael's sister Emily had been over from Dublin when I'd located Grandma's cottage at Christmas, and she'd provided me with details on Grandma's mysterious past.

A few months ago when Emily lost her caretaker, she hired Declan and offered to sell us the place. The recent sale of Declan's home, which he'd shared with his deceased wife, Shauna, had enabled us to jump at the chance to not only own the Daly house but also my Coffeys' cottage. Over the past year, I'd moved from a high-rise lake-front condo I'd shared with my emotionally abusive boyfriend, to my parents' tiny ranch house, to a studio apartment over Gerry's pub. Time for some stability.

This was where Declan and I would grow old together—next to Grandma's childhood home, where we first professed our love for each other.

I stepped from the car, and a tall patch of weeds brushed my leg. The head of the Tidy Town committee would be pounding on our door before long, reprimanding us about the overgrown lawn and dying bushes. On the man's first visit, he'd warned us that our place was keeping Killybog from winning Tidy Town of the year. Being at the village limits, we were visitors' first perception. We'd taken his kind *advice* and planted bushes in front of the house and flowers at the cottage. Yard maintenance was more time consuming than keeping up the house's interior.

In the distance sheep baaed, cows mooed, and a dog barked. Mac. His happy brown eyes peeked through the white lace curtains in the front peach-colored room. He disappeared, but his bark continued down the hall. I opened the door, and he jumped up, planting his furry tan paws on my chest, his tail wagging madly. He gave me kisses, and we nuzzled noses.

"Sit, Mac!" Declan commanded from the front room.

Mac sat his butt on the wooden floor, his tail still wagging.

"A good thing Daddy took over training you." I'd been a complete failure at it.

I rubbed the top of Mac's head. It was nice being greeted by my loving dog rather than Emily's grandfather's scary portrait, which had once hung on the former dark-green walls—now a creamy beige. The wealthy English landlord's crazy eyes would watch you. Mac had growled every time he'd walked past it, just like George's monkey table. Emily took all the scary family portraits so we could fill the walls with our own décor—like my portrait, which Declan had sketched in Prague, drawing for the first time since his muse, his late wife, had died nearly four years ago. The walls were still bare since we hadn't had time to decorate. Most of my stuff was in my apartment over Gerry's pub because all hell had broken loose after *Sunnyvale* aired, and our personal lives ceased to exist.

I joined Declan in the peach room, where he was standing at an easel by the tall front windows overlooking my Coffeys' home down the hill. The windows were open a crack to air the place out while keeping Mac in. A brisk wind blew inside and tousled Declan's brown hair, which nearly touched his shoulders. Caffeine from the empty Coke cans littering the surrounding floor lit his blue eyes. He had on my posh *La Haute Boheme* logoed velour robe and blue socks. Hopefully, he had on underwear. As much as I loved his naked butt...not on my luxurious robe. My naked butt only touched the robe after I'd showered, and it appeared that Declan hadn't showered since I'd left for England a week ago.

Still, I went over and gave him a hug and a fleeting kiss. Hmm... His lips tasted like cheese and onion Taytos.

"Be bringing out the animal in you even when I'm not showered, do I?"

I stepped back, sniffing the air. "Actually, I prefer your woodsy cologne. Right now you smell a bit too earthy. Like the inside of the Coffey cottage."

"That's brutal."

I glanced around at a dozen paintings propped up on the

green velvet couch and matching chairs. "Looks like you've been busy." They were copies of the woman writing a letter at the library desk, from George's wall. Prior to the *Sunnyvale* drama, an art enthusiast at a murder mystery event had admired the painting and paid Declan five grand for a copy. These smaller ones enabled him to crank them out faster and sell them for a more reasonable price. I hoped he didn't burn out, at the rate he was going.

"How'd Rachel be handling Gretchen stepping in for ya?"

"She was surprised."

"So was I."

"I'm a bigger person than you thought. Think this is going to be a good thing for Gretchen also, not just Rachel, and of course me. Gretchen needs a change and will hopefully decide to stay on." I eyed the empty Tayto wrappers littering the floor. "I was craving a Tayto sandwich. Would you like one if they're not all gone?"

"Sounds grand."

I snatched the paintbrush from his hand. "Go shower while I make lunch."

Mac followed Declan up the stairs, to nap on our bed, no doubt. On the way to the kitchen, I checked the mail on the hallway credenza, including a notice for my upcoming course in two weeks. It was rescheduled for January because the instructor was ill. I couldn't wait five months to add "educational background" to my résumé. I needed credibility now!

I slumped against the wall. I'd recently been rejected for a transcription project because they had too many volunteers. I couldn't even give away my time to gain experience. Despite Gretchen's envy over me pursuing my passion when she was burned out, I questioned if my career path was a mistake. Maybe there was a reason I kept getting sucked back into event planning. If Rachel discovered the class was canceled, she'd expect me to return to England. I had to enroll in an online course pronto and let Rachel believe it was in person. A virtual class would give me much-needed education but wouldn't provide networking opportunities as a way to land a job.

I entered the primrose-yellow kitchen Declan had painted to match Grandma's kitchen. The yellow apron I used to wear when helping her bake cookies hung on the wall next to the cream-colored cupboards. Sadly, the tile floor was still pea green. I despised peas. The refurbs, like our lives, were put on hold after the *Sunnyvale* episode.

I opened a bag of Taytos and stuffed a handful of chips into my mouth. I buttered four slices of brown soda bread, piled on the crisps, and slapped two slices of bread together. I flipped on the electric kettle on the countertop, and it hummed to life. I chose a teacup from my collection, one with a quaint stone bridge and scenic rolling green hills. My Flannery family's porcelain factory in County Wicklow had manufactured the cup, and an Irish cousin had given it to me. I dropped two teabags into my cup and a decaf bag into Declan's mug.

I was sitting on the couch in the peach room, enjoying my sandwich, when Declan came down from showering. He had on jeans and was slipping a white T-shirt over his bare, rock-solid chest with a dusting of brown hair. His freshly fallen rain-scented shampoo filled the air, as if blowing in through an open window. I eased out a contented sigh.

I tossed the cancelation notice onto the cocktail table.

"My class canceled. No instructor. Is the universe sending me signs that genealogy isn't my calling?"

"Right, then. Maybe it's telling you that you should take the next ferry back to England." Declan plopped onto the couch beside me. "You're not giving up that easily."

"See." I shook a crisp in my hand. "If I'm ready to give up that easily, maybe I'm not passionate enough about being a genealogist." Not as passionate as Gretchen thought I was. "Maybe my motivation to solve my grandma Coffey's family mystery was because it was personal."

"Look at the mystery you solved for Enid, and you hadn't a clue she was related to your Coffeys when you started researching."

"And I likely wouldn't have continued if I'd realized the road I was headed down."

"You would have. If you can earn a rave review on your website from nasty Enid, you've found your calling. Not to mention Gretchen also gave you one."

"Speaking of Gretchen, I wonder how things are going at the estate."

"No talking about the estate. We're taking the day off and spending it together." He leaned toward me and trailed warm kisses down my neck.

I let out a soft moan. "I have no plans until my genealogy meeting in the morning."

"Brilliant."

An arriving email dinged on my phone. I snatched it off the cocktail table.

Rachel.

My body tensed. She wondered if I preferred that Gretchen planned my wedding instead of her. I glared at the snarky email. "I don't want either you or Gretchen planning my stupid wedding!" I tossed the phone onto a pillow, my gaze darting to Declan's wounded look. "Sorry. Our wedding isn't stupid. I just don't want to get married at the estate, where everyone else wants me to. I'm all about family traditions, but not this one. If we have to move the wedding inside due to weather, no way am I walking down the same stairs as the actress and a bazillion fans. The stairs that chick tripped down and broke her wrist while taking a selfie. The estate is no longer the idyllic setting it once was." I shoved more crisps into my mouth.

As an event planner I always hoped for the best but planned for the worst. A pessimistic attitude for a bride-to-be.

"Better to have George and Fanny disappointed about not holding our wedding there than to have you disappointed by having it there. Let's elope." Declan stared at the sandwich in his hand. "To Paris, where we shared our first kiss."

Eloping seemed to have popped into Declan's head awfully quickly. Had he been considering it long?

Would I consider eloping? I hadn't a clue. The only thing I'd pictured about our wedding was tripping on my gown and falling down the stairs, thanks to that nightmare. When most women became engaged, they were out buying wedding planners and bridal magazines. I hadn't even looked at one while standing in line at a grocery store. Granted, I'd been crazy busy worrying about *clients'* weddings, yet it worried me I'd barely been thinking about my own!

"You want us to get married in the museum I was kicked out of twice? Don't think they'd allow it."

"We could still visit the Renoir exhibit where it all began."

I smiled. "I'd love to see Madame Laurent and Esme."

The boutique hotel owner and her dog had been my oasis in the middle of a brutal meeting in which I'd gained experience as a nanny rather than a planner. The trip I'd learned nappies and kids weren't in Declan's future. However, when I'd named our pet hen Henny Penny, a story he'd never heard of, I told him I'd have to be the one reading to our children. He'd looked intrigued rather than petrified at the thought of being a father. However, we'd never discussed having kids. Did I want kids?

"If not Paris, you pick the spot," he said. "I'm in as long as you're there. Just tell me when and where."

How about at the end of our drive at my Coffey cottage, where we'd first said I love you?

"Maybe we should take a nap and discuss it later." Declan gave me a sly grin followed by a passionate kiss.

Thoughts of weddings, kids, and Taytos drifted from my mind...

Three

THE SUN SHONE through the open bedroom curtains, brightening the navy walls, which would soon be a light spa blue. Hopefully, before long Declan would have time to paint walls rather than artwork. It was 8:00 a.m. We'd slept for ten hours—at least, Mac and I had. Declan was already up. I peered into my dog's big brown eyes, his head resting on Declan's pillow. I ruffled his tan fur, and he rolled onto his back, giving me his belly to rub. What a perfect way to wake up. No annoying 4:00 a.m. phone alarm demanding I drag my butt out of bed after only six hours of restless sleep. I snuggled with Mac and pushed thoughts of the estate from my mind.

"Morning, sunshine." Declan stood in the doorway, a shoulder relaxed against the frame.

I flashed him a flirty smile. "Would be even better if you came back to bed." I slipped my green *Coffey's Dublin* pub T-shirt over my head and tossed it onto the floor.

He slid a glance over his shoulder, untucking his white T-shirt from his jeans. "Best be quiet though. Don't want Michael to be hearing us."

"Michael?" I yanked the white duvet up under my chin. "Michael Turney?"

Declan nodded. "Called in to tell ya the genealogy meeting was canceled."

I groaned. "Doesn't that just figure. One more sign that—"

"You're becoming a Negative Nellie. You have a guest in the kitchen. Get dressed." A mischievous glint sparkled in his blue eyes. "Never told you to do that before, have I?" He walked out.

Mac and I sniffed the scent of bacon in the air. He sprang from the bed and followed Daddy to the kitchen. I hauled myself out of bed and pulled a pink T-shirt and faded jeans out of the antique wooden dresser. Emily had kindly left many of her furnishings.

I smiled at the framed photo on the dresser's lace scarf. A yellowed black-and-white one of Grandma and her sister Theresa in front of the Killybog church, wearing bright smiles and mid-length dresses. Cloche hats and light-colored, shoulder-length wavy hair framed their faces. Grandma had noted on the back that her dress was pink, her hat cream with a pink silk rose. Next to it sat Grandma and Michael Daly's engagement photo, taken in 1934. He had on a dark suit, and Grandma wore a white lace gown with a silver-and-emerald brooch pinned to the high-collared neck. Mom had worn the piece of jewelry for her wedding, as had Fanny for hers. I was next in line to wear the family heirloom. I brushed a gentle finger over the emerald brooch, lying on the dresser.

I headed down to the kitchen, where Declan was frying rashers in a pan on the large cast-iron stove. Mac sat patiently at his feet, hoping to be rewarded for his obedience. I said good morning to Michael—a thin gray-haired man in navy slacks and a white dress shirt seated at the table. His knotty-pine cane with a crack at the top rested across a chair. He'd inherited the walking stick from his cousin Nicholas Turney, my genealogy mentor, who'd sadly passed away the beginning of the summer. Nicholas had also left him shelves of genealogy and history books. Both men had been history professors.

"Sorry to hear your course in Dublin is on hold," he said. "I pray Martin will be on the mend soon and back to teaching by late autumn."

That was right. The instructor was a good friend of Michael's. Precisely why he'd recommended the ten-week intensive course on Irish records and research methodology. Thank God I hadn't whined about the class's cancelation.

"It's nothing too serious, I hope."

"Bad bout of pneumonia. He'll be grand." Yet concern deepened the wrinkles around the man's pale-blue eyes. "Since ya won't be taking the class, I thought you might be wanting a part-time position. My friend Winnie Dunne is recovering from cataract surgery and is in need of an assistant. She insists it's temporary. Doesn't want to be admitting she's slowing down even a wee bit." He gave me a wink.

Declan turned from the stove, metal spatula in hand. "An heir hunter, isn't she? Think I saw her on the tellie. Windiana Jones?"

I laughed. "Did you just make that up?"

"No. I swear that's her name."

"Aye, 'tis her nickname. She's quite the character. And quite lovely." Michael smiled. "Was given the name when her company, Genealogy Expeditions, was featured on a travel show."

"What exactly is an heir hunter?" I asked.

"She prefers to be called a probate genealogist. Heir hunters, like certain lawyers, could be termed as ambulance chasers. Many of them have a reputation for watching the obituaries and other sources for unclaimed estates so they can extort money from heirs in exchange for information on their inheritance. Winnie works on an hourly rate, not a percentage like some not-so-ethical firms known to charge up to forty percent."

Declan let out a low whistle. "That could be a load of quid, depending on the estate."

Michael nodded. "Indeed. She receives work from local authorities, nursing homes, hospitals, and solicitors. It's surprising how many people die without a will. Winnie is hired to verify the accuracy of existing family trees or has to build from scratch. She specializes in dinosaur cases, known as cold cases in the criminal field."

Declan smiled at me. "Sounds like fab experience."

I nodded. "And I could tell Rachel I have a job and can't be working afternoon teas." However, Nigel and Mindy hadn't yet responded to my plea for help.

"Even after recovering from her eye surgery, I think she'll still be needing help transcribing records and doing some of the legwork."

Being Windiana Jones's assistant would certainly sound impressive on my résumé.

"I'd love to meet her."

I'd envisioned Windiana Jones as a rugged, spry adventurer dressed in khakis and a brown leather jacket. I couldn't picture this petite, trim woman wrapped in a pink pashmina dodging poisonous arrows in her teal-colored sandals or swinging on a vine through the Amazon jungle without her long white hair becoming entangled in it. If the vine snapped, she'd drop to the ground and break every fragile bone in her body. However, the chunky stone pendant around her neck resembled a museum artifact that would keep the wisp of a woman from blowing off the Cliffs of Moher on a windy day.

"Mickey is a lovely man, but he needn't worry so much about me." Winnie brushed off his concern with a flutter of her ring-filled fingers. "I'll only be needing an assistant for a few weeks."

I pushed a yellow footstool out of the woman's way before she tripped over it.

"My eyesight is nearly back to normal."

Was *normal* legally blind?

"Your pashmina is beautiful," I said.

"Thanks, luv. From India. They have lovely clothing. Such bright colors."

Same as her décor. Colorful beaded pillows decorated a teal-colored couch that was a shade darker than the walls, which displayed artwork from her exotic travels. Recognizing the bridge in one, I walked over for a better look.

"The Charles Bridge in Prague," I said.

Where Declan had sketched my portrait and I'd scored art prints from a seller on the street. I'd been in the middle of negotiating with the man when a police officer came running toward us hollering out something in Czech. The guy took off, leaving me holding the prints. The officer raced after the man, and they disappeared around a corner. I'd gotten hot prints for free. One sold for about twenty-five bucks. Winnie's original painting had likely once hung in a Prague art gallery.

"Been there, have you?" she asked.

I nodded. "My most exotic trip."

"Prague is one of my favorite cities. So romantic."

"I was there for work, but my boyfriend did pop over for Valentine's Day."

I told her about my short-lived event planner career.

"You have a lifetime of adventures ahead of you, luv."

Speaking of adventures, next to the painting hung a framed photo of Winnie dressed in brown cotton pants, a weathered leather jacket, and an Indiana Jones–style hat. Precisely how I'd pictured the woman.

"Mickey might have mentioned my Windiana Jones feature on a travel show back when I had my Genealogy Expeditions company. I was a bit embarrassed about the whole gimmick being featured on the tellie, afraid it might ding my credibility. Instead, it launched my current career. A solicitor saw the show and contacted me to assist with locating heirs."

"What are you holding in the photo?"

"An old parish register that was locked away in a church basement in rural France. The holy grail that helped me solve a family mystery."

"So much can be found online now, I'm guessing you no

longer have to travel to search through old churches and archives."

"Nonsense. Ten percent of records and documents are online at best. Loads are located off the map, waiting to be uncovered." Winnie gazed off into space, a faraway look in her blue eyes. "As are the locals, who often hold more information than the archives. Your mission, should you choose to accept it..." Winnie chuckled. "Sorry. That's a line from the show *Mission Impossible*. Before your time."

"I know the movies." I'd rewatched the first one after my Prague meeting. The confectionary company's new product launch had identified plain-wrapper products with code names from the movie.

"I'll be needing help transcribing records online or at the archives, and also gravestones. Most importantly, buying pints for locals and area historians in the pubs to gather information."

"I think I can handle hanging out in pubs and chatting with the locals."

"I've solved more mysteries in pubs than I have in archives, thanks to a few pints. Have met some memorable characters."

"Do you do other jobs besides locating heirs?"

She shook her head. "That keeps me plenty busy. Many Irish die without a will and no known next of kin. It's rare that a bloodline dies out. It's just that the person fell out of touch with rellies, perhaps on purpose." Winnie relaxed in a purple velvet armchair. "Fancy a cuppa and some biscuits? The recipe is on the kitchen counter."

She expected me to bake cookies?

Winnie laughed. "Only messing, luv."

Dressing like Suzy Homemaker in an apron would be better than being dressed like a sausage.

The doorbell rang.

"Oh, that must be Fintan." Winnie sprang from her chair, nearly tripping over the footstool I'd moved out of her way. She squinted into a mirror on the wall, pinching color into her cheeks and brushing a hand over her long white hair. "See my lipstick anywhere, do ya?"

I found the tube on her desk, and she swiped a coral color across her lips. "The fella is quite the looker. Not as handsome as Mickey, but nice looking all the same. He's here about your jaunt to Scotland tomorrow."

"My jaunt to Scotland? Tomorrow?"

"If you accept the mission, that is."

The last thing I felt like doing was unpacking my suitcase so I could repack to fly to Scotland. Yet if I turned it down, my next trip would be back to England to help out at the estate. With any luck, Mindy and Nigel would accept my job offers.

"I'll take the job."

I hadn't a clue what the position paid, but working for the famous Windiana Jones would be a stellar reference and an awesome addition to my résumé. And I'd never been to Scotland. My previous employer, Flanagan Brewery, had canceled an incentive trip at a Scottish castle to go glamping in Galway. Zoe and I'd done the glamping site inspection, but luckily, I'd quit before the program.

Fintan Buckley was a tall, dapper-looking gray-haired gentleman dressed in a navy suit, white button-down oxford, and a navy-and-black tie. The man was quite a contrast to Winnie's colorful home. He placed a black leather hatbox with ivory trim on the desk. He flipped up the gold latch and opened the top to reveal a fancy magenta cloche embellished with lime-green flowers and colorful gemstones. My bridesmaid dresses would be the same purplish-pink color. My favorite.

I'd just made a decision for my wedding! Now I needed to figure out who the bridesmaids would be. Apparently I wasn't keen on eloping.

"My that's lovely, isn't it now?" Winnie said.

"It 'tis, isn't it?" Mr. Buckley smoothed a hand down his crisply pressed tie. "Not my colors, sadly." He let out a faint chuckle, which Winnie returned with a flirty giggle.

"I very much appreciate you assisting with the heirloom's delivery, Winnie."

"Why of course. No bother a t'all. My pleasure."

"Clara O'Shea wouldn't have trusted anyone else. Such a pity she has passed, or she'd be making the journey with you."

Winnie reached out to give him a comforting touch, but her hand missed his suit jacket sleeve by a few inches. "So sorry. I know the O'Sheas were one of your oldest clients."

"One of my first out of law school. Precisely why we are hand delivering the heirloom as requested." The man remained stoic. "Now then, here is the paperwork." He handed her a large brown envelope. "Patricia Muir will need to sign the letter of receipt, to be returned to me. The rest is hers to keep."

"No letter of authenticity or proof of insurance?" Winnie asked.

"None needed. It's a lovely hat but no real monetary value—merely sentimental."

Winnie had me snap a picture of the hat with my cell phone to confirm receipt of the family heirloom.

"Would you fancy a cuppa and some biscuits?" she asked.

"Wish I could, but I have a meeting to attend back in Dublin. Another time perhaps." He smiled.

Wearing a hopeful expression, Winnie watched the lawyer disappear out the door. She handed me the hatbox. "Treat as if it's the Holy Grail."

"Aren't you going with me tomorrow?"

"Haven't the time, luv. Have lots to catch up on after being out for my eye surgery."

"Will Mr. Buckley be upset if he finds out I went instead?"

"No worries, luv. I'll explain to Mrs. Muir I was in bad form and unable to travel. That hat is a blur of purple and green. With my poor eyesight, I can't be stumbling over suitcases and people in a busy airport. She'll be so happy to finally have the hat in her possession that she won't care one bit. And here." She slipped an autographed photo of herself into the envelope. "Told her I'd bring one along. She'd seen the show's episode and was quite excited when I offered her a snap."

"So was Mrs. Muir a close relation of Clara O'Shea?"

"She'd never heard of the woman before her death."

"Yet she's thrilled about getting the hat?"

"I've had people get excited about inheriting salt 'n' pepper shakers from Galway worth a few quid. It's often about them getting something when their relations received nothing." She rolled her eyes. "Family. Now, Mrs. Muir lives a two-hour train ride north of Edinburgh. You might be able to make the trip in one day if the flights and train schedules are timed just right. Otherwise, you'll need to be booking accommodations for the night. I promise to be giving you more than a day's notice when it comes to the Australia trip."

"Australia?"

That had to be at least a twenty-four-hour flight. Still, if I was traveling to gain genealogy experience, it'd be more bearable than meeting planning. And being on the other side of the world meant Rachel couldn't suck me back into working events. A one-night trip to Scotland was fine, but Australia would be much longer. A year ago when I was trying to escape my life, traveling was exciting. Now I had Declan, Mac, and our new home. I no longer wanted to escape. Except from England.

"No need to be giving me an answer on the Australia trip now, luv. We'd be making the trek together."

I pictured myself in the Australian outback traversing the rugged, non-crocodile-infested terrain in search of a remotely located church that held the key to our client's family mystery. The holy grail...

"I'll do it."

Winnie smiled. "Brilliant."

As much as I loved the photo of me in a blue beret and an *I Love Paris* T-shirt taken under the Eiffel Tower with Declan, I wanted some exotic and adventurous photos like Winnie's. Following Australia, I could see myself exploring the crypt of an old stone church in a remote French village... Scratch that. It had to be an English-speaking country so I could read the parish registers. Still, I could envision it.

Finally, I could picture my future.

Now, if I could just picture my wedding.

Four

BEFORE LEAVING WINNIE'S, I booked my flight to Edinburgh and a lovely B&B that she recommended in Old Town, the heart of the city. Winnie put everything on her credit card, so I didn't have to worry about expenses other than meals and incidentals. Back in my destitute event planner days, I had to juggle balances on my credit card and in my checking account, hoping I'd have enough to make it through a trip. I also learned that I would be earning twenty euros an hour and a three-hundred-euro-a-day flat rate when traveling. Not bad for my first job in the genealogy industry.

The only available nonstop flight Dublin to Edinburgh was the following day at noon. Rather than taking an expensive taxi from the airport to the city center, I planned to figure out the tram system, which made me nervous. However, I was paying attention to cost savings, like a responsible employee. A train arrived in Kilstruther two hours before the last train returned to Edinburgh. Plenty of time to drop off Mrs. Muir's hat and head back to Edinburgh. I had the next day to shop and tour the city before heading home. I wanted a unique souvenir to display in my new house. No tacky trinkets that ended up packed away in a closet. Of course, souvenirs didn't seem tacky until you got them home.

I parked in front of our house and checked an email from Mindy. She might have a canceled meeting, which would free her up next month for two weeks during the estate's back-to-back weddings. Too bad she wasn't able to hop a plane tomorrow. We'd still need her in a month though, so I asked her to keep me posted.

I planned to wait and tell Rachel about my new job, or it might send her over the edge again. Mom would be excited for me, but if I told her, she might slip up and tell my sister. I texted Gretchen to see if she was easing into her new position. I promised to return to the estate in a few days to give Fanny and George a break.

Mac was waiting for me at the door. Rather than nuzzling my nose and giving me kisses, he sniffed the hatbox. "There's no treats in there." I sniffed the air, filled with garlic and Italian spices floating down the hallway from the kitchen. Garlic bread and spaghetti. "I love your daddy."

Walking past the empty walls motivated me to pop by my apartment after returning from Scotland, to pick up my prints and sketch from Prague. Declan would be fine with me hanging them. My psycho ex-boyfriend had insisted on approving every print put on the wall. In the end, I'd sold an original painting by a Milwaukee artist on Craigslist, and...*Andy* had turned out to be the buyer. Thankfully, we'd met in a public place. He'd accused me of stealing *his* painting, causing me to second-guess myself, even though I knew damn well I'd bought it. He'd always played these mind games that had me questioning my decisions and abilities and ultimately my self-worth and sanity.

Thank God I'd escaped when I had.

As I passed the peach room, I peeked inside at stacks of boxed-up paintings ready to be shipped. In the kitchen Declan had a spoonful of red meat sauce for me to taste. Yum. I gave him a kiss. Mac barked for a bite.

"Sit," Declan commanded.

Mac obeyed, his tail slapping against the floor.

Declan gave him a tiny piece of browned hamburger he'd set aside when making the sauce.

I placed the hatbox on the table.

"Tell me about the famous Windiana Jones."

"Not what I'd expected." I described the woman and her eclectic décor. And that I was off to Scotland tomorrow. "Hopefully the job entails more experience than being a courier."

"Ah, that's grand. Congratulations." He gave me a kiss.

"You're okay with me going?"

"I promise to shower daily and to not be wearing your robe or your nightgowns."

Declan was joking about the nightgowns. I didn't own one except for a sexy little red one he'd never fit into. I wore my *Coffey's Dublin* T-shirt and leggings to bed.

"I'm a little nervous. The client expects Winnie to be delivering the hat, not me. Hope she doesn't get upset and call Mr. Buckley. Winnie didn't seem worried about it."

"Then you shouldn't be. She's the boss."

"What about me going to Australia for a few weeks? I told her I'd do it, but now I'm not sure."

Declan blinked in surprise. "That's a bit of haul, isn't it

now? I can't be promising you won't be finding me wearing your robe after that one, and eating all the Taytos. But ya should be doing it. Brilliant experience."

I nodded faintly.

"So what is this heirloom you're delivering?"

I opened the hatbox and revealed the magenta-and-lime-green hat. Mac hopped onto a chair for a closer look.

"Ah, that's lovely, isn't it now?"

A low growl vibrated at the back of Mac's throat and grew louder.

"Mac, it's just a hat," I said.

He sprang onto the table and attacked the heirloom.

"Mac, down!" Declan clapped his hands.

Mac released the hat, leapt from the table, and raced up the stairs, howling.

I snatched a napkin from the table and wiped off the saliva-covered jewels. No teeth marks had damaged the wool. I pointed out a flower with only two stones in the center. A half dozen others had three or four.

"Is there a gemstone missing?" I grabbed my phone from my purse and compared the photo of the hat to the actual one. "I should have taken one closer up. I can't tell if there was a stone there."

After searching the hatbox and floor for a sparkling green or purple stone, we flew upstairs and found Mac hiding under the bed. I ran down to the kitchen and grabbed his treats. I tossed one under the bed. He turned up his nose at it. I gave him another. He covered his eyes with a paw. Seriously? I went back down and washed the red sauce off several pieces of ground beef. I trailed bits of meat on the wood floor, leading him out from under the bed. He scarfed them down, and Declan scooped him up.

I gave Mac a stern look. "Who's training who here, mister?" I checked his mouth. No jewel. "What's the chance he swallowed one?"

"If he did, we should know within twenty-four hours." He set Mac down, and the dog scooted back under the bed undoubtedly expecting more treats before coming out.

"Should we wait that long? Maybe we should take him to the vet and have him x-rayed."

"If there *is* one in his stomach, are you going to be wanting the vet to operate?"

I gazed around frantically. "I don't know."

Declan placed his hands on my shoulders and gently massaged them. "Relax. My dog used to eat stones. I'm talking as big as a euro. The vet told us unless it was string, metal, or a sharp object, he'd be grand and eventually poop it out. And he always did."

"Then what? I take the jewel back to Mrs. Muir in Scotland and apologize that my dog just pooped it out? And would she like me to glue it back on to her hat?"

"I doubt he swallowed it. We're overreacting. And if he did, she won't even know it's missing."

I let out a distressed squeak.

"If I be ringing the vet, would ya feel better?"

I nodded. Being an event planner had taught me to be proactive, not reactive, whenever possible.

The vet advised us to keep an eye on Mac's stool for the next few days. Declan was on poop patrol while I was in Scotland.

The next day, an hour after the flight departed Dublin, the plane parked at the airport gate in Edinburgh. It was wonderful to no longer be afraid of the unknown and the craziness that would ensue the second I turned off my cell phone's airplane mode and was bombarded with notifications. Flying for work and dealing with delays and cancelations had been the most peaceful part of the job because nobody could reach you.

I turned on my phone. Not one message.

Nigel, Rachel, or Gretchen hadn't reached out to me.

What was up with that? There was no making me happy.

Mom hadn't contacted me in a while either. When I first started traveling, she'd text or call a half dozen times a day. Then I moved above Gerry's pub, and she started calling him to check on me. It was weird that I hadn't heard from her in at least a week. No call wondering if I'd confirmed a wedding date or if I'd invited Uncle Benny despite his crude jokes. I'd have to phone her later when I had more time to chat.

I texted Fanny the picture of the hat. Moments later she replied that she adored it, even if it wasn't her favorite blue. She thought she'd even seen it somewhere.

Maybe I could borrow a hat from Fanny for my wedding, except I'd never seen her wear magenta. She'd have something blue I could borrow. Idea number two and three.

A ding filled the air, and I smiled at my phone.

An email from Rachel. She was concerned that I hadn't chosen a wedding date. Not because she was worried that I no longer wanted her to plan the wedding, but was I having second thoughts about marrying Declan? If I was, that was just natural. She was there if I needed to talk.

If I'd remained in event planning, I'd have become a paranoid, neurotic pessimist like my sister. I was already well on my way, freaking out that I couldn't envision my wedding, which was why I hadn't confirmed a date.

I tucked my phone back into my purse and headed up the aisle. When I'd boarded, the overhead bin space in the back was full, so I'd stored my carry-on and hatbox four rows ahead of me. I grabbed my purple bag and went to grab the hatbox. No hatbox. Heart racing, my gaze darted around, landing on a navy hatbox with tan trim two rows up. I spied a woman in a black-and-white polka-dot dress exiting the plane carrying my black hatbox.

"Wait! That's my hatbox!"

The woman disappeared out the doorway.

I grabbed the navy case from the bin and bolted toward the exit. What was the chance of there being two hatboxes on the same flight? Two similar-looking hatboxes on top of it? Granted, hats were much more common in Ireland and Scotland than in the US, yet still, I couldn't recall ever having seen a hatbox in an overhead bin. I raced off the plane and up the jet bridge into the busy terminal.

The woman and a man in a black suit were clipping along on the white tiled floor. I weaved in and out of the crowd with my small carry-on bag bouncing along on its wheels behind me.

"Stop the lady with the hatbox!" I yelled out. "Stop the woman in the polka-dot dress!"

People were *stopping* to stare at the crazy woman shouting out demands.

The couple came to a halt for a beeping cart transporting a passenger, enabling me to catch up with them.

"Excuse me." I gasped for air. "That's my hatbox."

The woman glanced down at the black case. "Oh my, so it is. So sorry. How did I manage to do that?"

"Because you have more hatboxes than purses." The man had his back turned to me, checking his phone. "It's impossible to keep them all straight, luv."

"So sorry again."

We exchanged cases, and I about collapsed with relief, hugging the hatbox against my chest. The scent of nutmeg filled my head, bringing back memories of Grandma's maple nutmeg cookies. I relaxed my hold on the case and glanced around. No bakery, only a coffee shop making fancy cappuccinos and lattes. My stomach grumbled.

The couple continued on their journey.

Some things never changed. Same as meeting planning, nothing ever went as planned. No matter what happened this trip, it couldn't be as stressful as working an event. Windiana Jones was about to launch my genealogy career. I could feel it...and see it. I pictured myself driving through the vineyards of Tuscany searching for a small stone church with old parish registers stored in the medieval building's wine cellar.

Mmm... I could also taste it.

Five

I WAS BACK on track after the hatbox fiasco. Catching the tram from the airport to the city-center train station had gone smoothly. A lovely uneventful two-hour train ride through Scotland's green rolling countryside was a relaxing journey, with my hands gripping the gold handle of the hatbox on my lap. I texted Zoe my idea about wearing a hat for my wedding. My friend was mad about hats. Last Christmas Declan had bought her a small red hat with a cluster of red maple leaves on one side. A replica of the one Kate, the Princess of Wales, wore to the Queen's River Pageant and on her visit to Canada. Zoe had worn it to Christmas Mass, and I'd worn her purple lacy hat. I was fairly certain that was the last time I'd worn a fancy hat. What if I wasn't comfortable wearing one and spent all day fussing with it?

Within a half hour Zoe was texting photos of glamorous magenta-colored hats with foofy feathers, flowers, bows... Mac would go wild over the hats. I replied that I had something a bit more simplistic in mind that Mac wouldn't shred to bits or bark at through the entire wedding ceremony. And one without a wide brim so it wouldn't be difficult for Declan to kiss me.

She was on it.

Mostly fishing boats filled the small village's marina. Pubs, seafood restaurants, and fish markets lined the main street, providing views of the North Sea stretching across to Norway and Denmark. I headed up a shaded side street, leaving behind the sunshine and brisk winds blowing a fishy smell off the water.

Mrs. Muir's was a quick ten-minute walk from the train station. Two hours and I'd be hopping the last train into Edinburgh and would spend the evening exploring quaint shops and art galleries for the perfect souvenir. I assured myself that if she examined the hat closely, she wouldn't notice a missing gem because they were all intact. No way had Mac swallowed a gemstone. Had he? Declan was keeping an eye out for sparkly poop. If a stone appeared, we agreed it would remain missing. At the moment I was more worried that Patricia Muir would be upset that she was missing her opportunity to meet a celebrity, Windiana Jones. In all fairness to Winnie, traveling had to be difficult with her poor eyesight. The fact that she hadn't told Fintan Buckley that I would be delivering the heirloom shouldn't be a ding to her moral work ethic. Yet it bugged me.

Patricia lived in a row of stone townhouses with colorful doors. Red and yellow pansies lined the path to her purple door. A petite, plump, seventy-ish-year-old woman with short white hair greeted me with a bright smile.

"I can't believe it's finally arrived." The woman was breathing heavy and wiping sweat from her brow. "Sorry.

Just back from my morning walk. Do come in, luv." She ushered me into a small entryway with light-sage walls and white trim.

I handed off the hatbox, relived it was no longer my responsibility.

"My mum never mentioned a Clara O'Shea in Ireland. Maybe she'd never heard of her either. Guess we'll never know."

A sense of pride brought a smile to my face. Helping people discover relations and learning their family history was a rewarding career.

The woman moved aside several pictures of couples, children, and dogs on a white credenza, making space for the hatbox. One of a wedding couple caught my eye. The bride had on a cocktail-length 1920s-style flowing dress. It reminded me of the photo with Grandma and her sister in front of the church.

I pictured myself wearing a similar dress at my wedding...

Mrs. Muir opened the case, unveiling the cloche. She snapped a hand to her chest. "It's simply lovely, isn't it? Thanks so much for delivering it, luv. Lime green is my favorite color. It's a sign—I know it is. I'll wear the hat to the races this weekend and have a windfall. Someone is watching over me." She glanced upward. "Pastor Archie said the same. He's even having me place a few quid on a pony." She smiled at the hat. "It's sure to be my lucky hat."

"It certainly is your lucky day, discovering a relation you never knew existed. Learning about my Irish grandmother's past changed my entire future. I've obtained Irish citizenship, moved to her homeland, and am engaged to the Irish love of my life."

The woman's face lit up, and she grasped hold of my arm. "*Lover* Boy. It's another sign. His odds are eighty to one. A real long shot I never would have placed a bet on." She glanced toward the ceiling. "This can't be a coincidence, can it?"

She was betting on a long shot because I'd mentioned marrying the love of my life?

"Um, I just need you to sign a receipt." I slipped the large brown envelope from my purse. When removing the needed paperwork, a white stationary envelope addressed to *Patricia Muir* in shaky handwriting fell to the floor. A letter from Clara O'Shea? I snatched it off the blue throw rug and slipped it back inside the larger envelope. "If you could please just sign this paper confirming receipt."

"Certainly, luv." She jotted her name on the line.

"And this is an autographed photo from Windiana Jones. I'm sorry that she—"

"Didn't realize I'd inherited a celebrity photo also. This really is my lucky day. Have much value, does it?"

"No. Windiana Jones was on that travel show you used to watch."

She nodded faintly.

"It's thanks to Winnie that you were located."

"Oh my, that's right. I'd forgotten that in all the hat excitement."

Guess Winnie had overstated her popularity.

I slipped the photo back inside the envelope. "An O'Shea family biography is also included." Hopefully, a family member would care more about their family history than this woman did.

"Wish I could have you in for tea, luv, but my family will

be calling in soon to see the hat. Here's a little something for your journey home." She slipped a silver coin from her pocket and handed me a pound.

Gee, I could celebrate my trip with a shot of cider.

"Good luck on the ponies."

She placed the hat on her head and admired it in the mirror over the credenza. "I look like a winner, don't I, luv?"

I guess it was her loss not caring more about the family history than the hat. It still made me sad.

Relaxing in a pub's window booth, I toasted a cider to my first solo trip. Outside of the small snafu with the switched hatboxes, the trip had been seamless despite involving three modes of transportation. Taking a sip of the sweet apple-flavored beverage, I sank back against the wooden bench, watching the boats in the marina bobbing in the water. In a celebratory mood, I brushed off the fact that Patricia Muir cared more about winning loads at the track than inheriting a family heirloom.

A painting of seagulls hung on the pub's paneled wood walls along with fishing nets, colorful glass fishing floats, and black-and-white photos tracing the pub's history as well as the village's. I took another sip of cider. Just over an hour until the train back to Edinburgh and I'd be browsing galleries for a reasonably priced piece of artwork.

A man entered the pub dressed in green wellies, oversized oilskin trousers, and a cream wool sweater. He went straight to the bar. "Have ye heard Mrs. Muir had a massive heart attack, she did." His gruff, booming voice filled the empty bar.

"Nay, died, did she?" The gray-haired bartender, dressed in a black T-shirt, poured the man a pint.

He shrugged. "Paramedics were there. Dunno how she's fairing."

Muir was likely a common Scottish surname, right?

I went over to the bar. "You're not talking about Patricia Muir, are you?"

"Aye, knew her, did ya, lassie?" the fisherman asked.

The bartender smacked the man's arm. "Ya be sounding as if the woman is dead. Don't be starting rumors."

"I, ah, just met her," I said.

So much for her new lucky hat.

Another man came in wearing a red windbreaker with silver reflective stripes and a *Royal Mail* logo on the back. "Did ye hear—"

"Aye, we heard," the fisherman said.

"Just saw her when I was making a delivery." The man eyed me. "Didn't I see ya calling in on her?"

I nodded.

"American, are ya?" he asked.

I nodded again. "I live in Ireland."

"What were ya doing there?"

"Delivering a package."

The postman's gaze narrowed. "What company ya be working for?"

"That's confidential."

"Not such a secret that ya shouldn't be telling Detective Orr."

"Er, he's right," the bartender said. "Ya should be letting

him know you were likely the last one to be talking to her. Not that she isn't still alive, but ya know what I mean."

"I'll go see the detective."

I took another gulp of cider and headed out the door, off to clear my name from any involvement in the woman's heart attack. When I'd arrived at her house, she'd been a bit out of breath. However, she'd seemed fine when I'd left. Maybe the excitement of winning big on a long shot had been too much for the older woman's heart.

I hoped she was still alive. Not to sound callous, but what happened to the hat if she did die? Was it my duty to return it to Mr. Buckley or leave it here to become part of her estate? Would it go to one of her children, if she had children, or another relation? She'd mentioned family coming to see her new heirloom. Family needed to know the history behind the hat so it didn't end up at a thrift shop.

I called to ask Winnie about protocol and got her voicemail.

"Sorry 'bout missing your call. I'm out bothering the living, trying to find the dead. Please leave a message, and I'll ring ya back."

I turned the corner to see a flash of green-and-yellow stripes as the ambulance sped away. A police vehicle remained parked at the road. Locals congregated on the sidewalk in front of the house, speaking in hushed tones. I marched past them and up the path, as if the detective had requested my presence. I stepped inside, where a middle-aged man in jeans and a lightweight blue sweater peered at me from behind wire-framed glasses.

"Can I help you?" He sounded more annoyed than eager.

I explained that the lads at the pub had suggested I tell him about my visit with Patricia Muir.

"I wasn't here more than ten minutes. When I got here, she was a bit out of breath having just returned from a walk. She seemed perfectly fine when I left. Excited about the inheritance and wearing the hat to the races this weekend. She was sure it was going to bring her luck betting on the ponies."

He let out a faint laugh. "God love the woman, but she's frugal. Never gambled a day in her life."

"She knew an awful lot about horse betting for not being a gambler. She even planned on placing a bet for Reverend Archie."

"Reverend Archie?"

I shrugged. "From her church, I assumed."

"The local minister is Reverend Campbell. That's him with her in the snap." He gestured to the picture of a minister and a tall, trim woman with short white hair.

My gaze narrowed on the photo. "That's not Mrs. Muir."

"I assure you that is indeed Patricia Muir. I've known the woman since she taught me in primary school."

I walked over to the photo for a closer look. "Well, *I* assure you that isn't the woman I gave the hat to a half hour ago." However, this woman looked like the one in several of the photos on the entryway credenza.

"Certain you're at the right house, are ya?" He sniffed the air. "Had a pint or two down at McWattie's pub?"

I squared my shoulders in defense. "I'd had a few swallows when I heard about Mrs. Muir and came straight here to do my civic duty and provide any information I can."

The detective quirked a brow. "So another woman

supposedly answered that door, and you didn't see Mrs. Muir the entire time you were here?"

"Not *supposedly*. That other woman did answer the door." I went over to the entry and reenacted the entire scene from the time I'd arrived, handed off the case, and left. "I never went any farther than the foyer with that yellow-painted coatrack and white wooden credenza."

"The houses in this row all look the same. Maybe you delivered the hat to the pink door instead of the purple one."

I was questioning myself.

He glanced around. "So where is this hat?"

My gaze darted around the room. "Good question. Is it okay if I look for it?"

"Aye, please do."

I searched the entire place and came up empty, including no large brown envelope. However, poor Winnie's photo was sticking out of the kitchen garbage bin. I wouldn't mention that a thief hadn't felt her photo was worth stealing. However, the fake Mrs. Muir had snatched the envelope with the family history and handwritten letter. Why would a thief care about those?

"The hat's not here. Neither is the paperwork."

"What paperwork?"

"A history on the decedent Clara O'Shea's family and a handwritten letter, I'm guessing from her also. No letter of authenticity or proof of insurance was needed. Her lawyer hired my boss to track down the heir. That's what Winnie does. She's an heir hunter, er, probate genealogist. Here's a photo of her I found, proving I was indeed in this house."

The detective's gaze narrowed on Winnie's adventurer

pic. "Windiana Jones is your boss? Where's your office? In an Amazon hut or Egyptian tomb?"

I gave him an unamused smile. "She's a renowned genealogist. This was merely an outfit she wore when she escorted genealogy expeditions and appeared on an episode of some travel show."

He raised a skeptical brow.

"Why would I be making up a story like this? *How* could I even make up a story like this?"

"Aye, good question."

I pulled up her website on my phone. The home page included dozens of testimonials and links to prestigious magazine articles and video clips about her.

He let out a defeated grunt. "What did this hat look like?"

I sent him the photo of it.

"This thief was a bit incompetent if she left the computer, TV, and a jewelry box in the bedroom and took a hat not worth insuring."

I shrugged. "Maybe she thought a letter of authenticity or insurance papers were in the envelope. Even if the hat has little value, perhaps Mrs. Muir led people to believe it had and told that to the wrong person. As a retired schoolteacher, she might have been wanting to sound like she had a bit of excitement in her uneventful life. I still think it has something to do with the paperwork."

Besides family members, who would care about the family history or Clara O'Shea's letter?

I had copies of letters from Grandma's sister Theresa. Grandma had read the originals so many times that the folds on the yellowed pages were worn through, making the words on the creases difficult to read. They hadn't held any clues to Grandma's past and mainly discussed people we'd assumed were their siblings or Theresa's children. Seeing your ancestors handwriting and imagining them penning the letter all those years ago was an emotional experience.

I cherished those letters.

"I'm guessing the thief figured the hat was valuable or wouldn't have risked getting caught and leaving Mrs. Muir here to possibly die," he said.

"Did Patricia call 999 herself?"

"Not sure. A call came in from here approximately forty-five minutes ago, around the same time you were here." He gave me a curious look. "Nobody was on the line."

"Well, I didn't make the call."

I'd like to think the impersonator had at least dialed for help before she left Mrs. Muir on the floor to die.

"Our client works for a very reputable firm. If the hat were valuable, I would have been informed so I could have been extra cautious. Actually, if it was that valuable, they wouldn't have sent *me* to deliver it. They'd have hired a security firm."

However, I wasn't supposed to have been delivering it —Winnie was.

"This impersonator obviously knew the hat was being delivered today," I said. "Mrs. Muir likely told family and friends about it."

"You're saying a *friend* left her to die on the living room floor while she impersonated her, then stole a hat of no value?"

What if that poor woman had been lying on the floor

dying the entire time I'd been chatting with the impostor about the hat?

"Maybe the mystery woman came here for a visit, found Mrs. Muir on the floor, and thought she was dead. Then I showed up with the hat she presumed was valuable, so impersonated Mrs. Muir. If Mrs. Muir died, the hat would go to her heir. Does she have any children?"

He nodded. "A daughter in Australia."

"Maybe the thief is a family member and thought she was more deserving of the hat than a child who lived thousands of miles away. Family members fight over salt 'n' pepper shakers from Galway, for God's sake."

"Do you have a copy of the signed paperwork?"

I showed him the receipt with the illegible signature.

"This is helpful." He handed it back to me. "You'll need to go to the station and give a description of the impostor to Mrs. Foster."

I glanced at the clock on the wall. "My train leaves in forty minutes. It's the last one to Edinburgh."

"I'll ring her now and see if she's available. School isn't in session, so hopefully she's around."

"She's a teacher?"

He nodded. "Can't be affording to keep a sketch artist on the payroll in this small town."

She better draw fast!

I asked the detective to please keep me posted on Mrs. Muir's condition and left for the police station. Heading down the path, I encountered a gentleman wearing a concerned expression, black slacks, and a white oxford. His gaze darted from the police vehicle at the road to Patricia's house.

"What's happened? Is Patricia all right?"

"Are you a relative?"

He nodded. "Her nephew."

"She's been taken to the A and E. It appears she had a heart attack." A warm vanilla scent filled my head, and my stomach growled. I should have had chips with my cider.

He snapped a hand to his chest. "Bloody hell. A heart attack?"

"So sorry. The detective inside can tell you more."

"I need to get to the hospital." He turned and rushed off.

There was something familiar about him. Had he been walking around town, at the pub, or on the train... It didn't matter. I needed to call Winnie and get to the police station so I'd make the last train to Edinburgh.

What if Winnie or Mr. Buckley thought I'd stolen the hat rather than delivering it since this was my first day on the job? Suddenly I agreed with Winnie about not telling the lawyer that I'd delivered the hat instead of her! Thankfully, I had a signature on paper to prove it. An illegible signature of a possible killer. I should have asked Mrs. Muir for identification. Who knew some other woman would be answering the door? Another lesson learned the hard way.

Six

"Oh, that poor woman," Winnie said. "Maybe the shock of it all was just too much for her heart. Hope she doesn't die before learning the truth and..."

"What truth?"

Silence filled the line.

"Um, not the *truth*. Rather, the *details* about the O'Shea family history." Winnie cleared her throat. "Right, then. Might be Patricia Muir asked that other woman, a friend or rellie, to speak with you on her behalf because she was lying ill in bed and wasn't up to signing the form. Yet it doesn't make sense that the hat is missing while Mrs. Muir remained lying on the floor, nearly dead. Still think a rellie is somehow involved. I've seen them get in fierce brawls over a new teacup with no sentimental or monetary value. People lose their wits and become completely mad after a death in the family. Not a good first day for you, was it, luv?"

"Could have been better."

"I promise nothing like this has ever happened before."

If I quit, I would have to return to the estate. This had to be a one-off. The woman didn't call herself Windiana Jones because she was dealing with things like this all the time, did she?

"Your next task will be uneventful. A quick trip to Donegal to transcribe gravestones. What could be more peaceful than a day in the cemetery? I should ring Fintan and let him know what has happened. It's out of our hands at this point. All we can do is say a prayer for Patricia Muir and keep Fintan updated on her condition and the hat's investigation. Your job is done."

"I hope he's not upset that you didn't deliver it and that he believes I *did* deliver it. Being my first day, he might think I'm not to be trusted and stole it."

"He'll think no such thing, luv. Besides, he'll know this likely isn't about the hat."

"What do you mean?"

Winnie let out an indecisive groan. "The details of the case are confidential. I need to be checking with Fintan before sharing any information. I'll ring ya back tonight. Now, off to the police station so you can be making the last train."

Click.

What was that about?

I came to an abrupt halt at a corner, peering down the street for the sea in the distance. I clipped along in the direction of the police station located on the waterfront road, calling Declan.

"Has Mac pooped out a gemstone yet?" I asked straight off.

"Right, then. You're sounding a bit desperate for him to

be pooping out something we aren't even sure he swallowed."

"I'm worried about him." And I wanted to prove to the snarky detective that the thief was ultimately after the paperwork and not the hat. I explained the situation. "I want to prove Mac's poop isn't worth a fortune."

"Jaysus, Caity. You best be getting to the train station straight away. If someone attempted to kill that woman and stole the hat, you can identify her, and she knows it."

"If I don't go to the police station to give a description, it'll look suspicious. And the detective will come find me. Besides, I need to help if I can. What if the woman dies? She deserves justice and so do I. It ticks me off that I was duped my first day on the job."

"Well, ya better make that train. If not, I'm coming over."

"That's crazy. It'd take you eight hours to get here between driving to the airport, flying over, and hopping a train or renting a car."

He sighed in defeat. "Suppose Rachel is closer if you need someone."

I'd rather be stalked by a possible killer than go back to the estate.

"She doesn't know I'm here. I'm not about to tell her until I get home, or she'll be calling every five minutes to make sure I'm okay. She'll drive me nuts."

"Change your flight to the earliest one out in the morning."

"I'm going to, believe me. I guess we can scratch Scotland off our list of possible places to elope."

Declan wasn't amused. He also didn't provide any

further insight into his opinion on eloping and if he was seriously considering the option.

This was the first time I'd traveled solo in a foreign country without relations or coworkers nearby to have my back. However, Declan would always have my back no matter where I was in the world.

#

I studied Gracie Foster's sketch of the petite, plump older woman with short white hair, blue eyes, and a deceivingly pleasant smile.

"That's her. The woman who pretended to be Patricia Muir. Does she look familiar to you?"

The woman's white eyebrows narrowed, her grip tightening on her pencil. "Sadly, no. Wish she did. Still can't imagine such a horrible thing happened to poor Patricia. We taught together for nearly forty years. I started a year before her."

"Do you know if she'd had heart problems?"

Gracie shook her head. "But that was the thing everyone loved about Patricia. She was always so pleasant. Not a negative thing to say about anyone. When she comes out of surgery, she'll put on a sunny smile and say how lovely the doctor and nurses were, the hospital food was delightful, and her bed the comfiest ever." She choked back a sob. "My niece works at the hospital and said she's been in surgery for an hour—it sounds quite serious."

I placed a hand on the woman's arm. "She'll be fine. Optimists put less stress on their bodies than pessimists, making them healthier and better able to recover from emotional and physical trauma. And she has her nephew and family waiting for her when she comes out of surgery."

Gracie dabbed the tears from her eyes with a tissue. "Outside of her daughter in Australia, she only has a distant cousin in Wales she barely knows. That's one reason she was so excited to learn about the hat and a distant relation in Ireland. Even though that woman had passed, Patricia held out hope there were others who she might meet."

That was the Patricia I wanted to meet.

"What about her nephew?" I asked.

She shook her head. "She had no siblings—neither did Nick, her husband. What made you think she has a nephew?"

The man who'd claimed to be her nephew at her house.

I told Gracie about the distraught gentleman I ran into rushing up the walk toward Patricia's house.

"Well, that's certainly odd. First someone impersonating dear Patricia and then someone claiming to be her nephew?"

It certainly was odd.

With a determined look, Gracie poised her pencil against a clean sheet on her sketch pad. "What did this man look like?"

I was never going to make that last train.

I described the tall, handsome man with green eyes... The scent of Grandma's maple nutmeg cookies filled my head. Omigod! The guy from Mrs. Muir's was the same one from the airport! The man's cologne or shampoo smelled like a mix of nutmeg and warm vanilla. Grandma's cookies!

"I saw him earlier today at the Edinburgh airport. I'm sure of it. Well, almost. I didn't get as good a look at him at the airport." I told her about the hatbox switch.

"That certainly couldn't have been a coincidence."

"I didn't get a great look at him at the airport, but I smelled him."

The woman gave me an odd look.

"He smelled like my grandma's maple nutmeg cookies."

"Oh, those sound lovely. Don't find many maple-flavored sweets here."

My stomach growled. I was going to bake Grandma's recipe even if it caused a panic attack after this whole ordeal.

Had the couple followed me on the plane and also the train, waiting for the opportune moment to steal the hat again? Yet they couldn't have relied on a "getaway" train, not on the limited schedule in this remote village. So if the man had driven here, how had I beat him when the train made at least a half dozen stops? I didn't have to worry about them now, because I no longer had the hat. Unless they thought *I'd* stolen it!

I had to watch my back.

The door to the station opened, startling me.

The detective came to a halt. "A wee bit on edge, are ye?"

"Sorry. I was afraid you were Mrs. Muir's nephew."

"Woman didn't have a nephew." He glanced over at Gracie. "Did she?"

Gracie shook her head. "She most certainly did not."

I told him about my two encounters with the mystery man who claimed to be a nephew. "Not only was someone impersonating Mrs. Muir but also her nephew, which of course I hadn't a clue she had no nephew at that time. But how had *he* known I didn't have a clue unless he knew who I was?"

"Because you're American, not local?" the officer said.

"Doesn't mean I don't know Mrs. Muir on a personal basis. Oh, and he was with a woman at the airport, but I didn't see her here in town."

If she was interested in the handwritten letter or family history, then why had she taken the hatbox? She must have assumed the envelope was in the case. At least I'd done the smart thing without even knowing it, keeping the hat and paperwork separate.

The detective looked intrigued. "You're sure the man at the airport and Mrs. Muir's was the same one? You saw him clearly both times?"

I nodded with a slight shrug. "Pretty much. Granted, I didn't get the best look at him at the airport, but the two men were Irish with the same build and had on the same black pants. Both times I'd seen him, I'd craved my grandma's maple nutmeg cookies. It's his cologne—I'm sure of it."

"Maybe both men wear the same cologne."

"I haven't craved those cookies in years. What's the chance I would crave them twice in one day?"

He looked skeptical but told Gracie to draw the couple.

For sure I wasn't making the last train.

"Mrs. Muir will always be an A-plus lady in my book." The rugged-looking man sitting at MacWattie's bar raised his pint.

A man clinked his glass. "Even though I'm sure ya never got an A in her class."

"Or a B," another chimed in.

"I'll have ye know I earned good marks. She was always a fair teacher."

I showed the bartender my photos of Gracie's sketches of the two impersonators and the woman at the airport.

"Can't say I'd be recognizing any of 'em. Sorry, lassie." He passed my phone to the man across the bar, who shook his head like all the others. "Look like ya be needing a cider." He poured me a pint. "On the house."

"Thanks." The line of men at the bar passed my phone back down to me. "I didn't figure a local would have been bold enough to commit a crime or to leave that poor woman lying on the floor in need of medical attention."

The bartender nodded. "If she weren't such a lovely woman, I'd be wondering if maybe someone had intended her harm and merely wanted to make it look like a theft by nicking that hat you were talking about."

I assumed it was okay to talk about the hat. Not like I'd divulged any major details about the crime. Showing the locals a pic might help in case someone saw a woman walking around wearing the hat or found it tossed in a rubbish bin in an alley. And I agreed. The woman was well liked. That wasn't always the case with a schoolteacher. One of my favorite teachers was Mrs. Simpson. She'd given me an A in creative writing for my paper on how to catch a cat thief. It was based on our cat Izzy, and many of the adventures were inspired by real ones. Like the time she'd come inside after being sprayed by a skunk and we chased her all over the house, then outside, where she climbed a ladder into the attic over the garage and we found my missing hair clip, the head of Rachel's Barbie doll, and Mom's gold chain.

Too bad it wouldn't be that easy to solve this mystery.

The door opened, startling me. A brisk wind and the uniformed postman blew in. He gave me a nod hello.

No clue why I was so on edge. It wasn't like that fake nephew and Mrs. Muir had stuck around. They had no reason to be stalking me now that they had the hat. Or at least one of them had the hat. I assumed they were in it together.

"I think I'll take my glass to go," I told the bartender.

Five minutes later I was opening my guest room door above the bar, overlooking a sketchy alley and brick building. I snapped the blue curtains shut. My aunt Dottie had been mugged while studying abroad in London thirty-one years ago, so the first time I'd gone to Dublin, Mom had insisted I pack defense spray. Too bad I hadn't packed it this trip. I took a gulp of cider. I hadn't heard from Winnie. Maybe she was waiting to hear back from Fintan to verify if she could divulge the case's background and if he had a copy of the handwritten letter. I didn't want to call and bug her about it. She'd get in touch with me.

My phone shrilled, about catapulting me through the ceiling. Declan. I cleared my throat, took a deep breath, and answered it with a perky hello.

"We have a winner. Mac pooped out an emerald."

"Is he okay?"

"He's grand. Knew he'd done it because was barking like mad where he'd gone in the yard. I'll pop into Mullingar tomorrow. There's a jeweler who I'm sure can confirm it's fake."

I told Declan about the supposed nephew and missing the last train to Edinburgh because I had to provide details for two additional sketches.

"Jaysus, Caity, ya need to be getting out of there. Now."

"Unless I can hire a fisherman to take me down the coast to Edinburgh, that isn't happening. And I nearly got sick on the large ferry that one time coming over. I'd be puking my guts out on a fishing boat."

"Reminds me of the time I took a group deep-sea fishing off the northern coast of Scotland. The charter company recommended we buy plenty of motion-sickness meds to hand out. I was so busy making sure everyone took the bloody yokes so I wouldn't be cleaning up vomit that I forgot to be taking one myself. I retched all over an attendee's new wool fisherman's sweater. The man went absolutely mad. Thought he was going to toss me overboard and I'd end up on the Shetland Islands."

I laughed. Declan always had a story about his own mishaps to make me feel better.

"Even if you retch down the entire coast, at least you'd be out of that Cabot Cove of Scotland."

"You know *Murder, She Wrote*?"

"My mum watched it."

"Ahh. Kind of like George claiming he'd never seen an episode of *Sunnyvale*."

"Don't change the subject."

"What was I supposed to do? I had to give the descriptions to the sketch artist."

"I'm meeting you at the Dublin airport tomorrow morning and following you home. I should have flown over. Promise me you'll go straight from the train station to the airport."

"I already booked the first flight out in the morning. I'll send you the details. I just can't believe that poor woman might have been lying on the floor fighting for her life the entire time I was standing in the entryway. If only I'd gone inside—"

"You might also be in the A and E. No way am I losing the second woman I've ever loved."

"You're not going to lose me. I love you too." I made smoochie sounds and promised to phone him when I was en route tomorrow.

I wasn't qualified to find a criminal. Macarons was one thing, a criminal another. Had the couple known *I* was bringing the heirloom from Dublin today, or had they merely been looking for someone carrying a hatbox boarding a plane from Dublin to Edinburgh? They had Irish accents and could have been O'Shea relations. I didn't know where to begin looking for these people, and hopefully, they didn't know where to look for me.

I dropped onto the bed and snatched the pint off the end table. My phone rang. Nigel.

I answered with an enthusiastic hello.

"Miss Caity. Your email was a lovely surprise, my dear."

"Does that mean you're interested in the job? Please tell me yes. At least the weddings."

"Your timing is impeccable. I could use a reprieve from my lovely yet cantankerous aunt."

"Wonderful." I collapsed back on the headboard with a sense of relief, steadying my pint. "I'm in Scotland right now. I'll give you a call when I get home tomorrow, to discuss the position."

"You're in Scotland? Whatever for?"

"Scotland!" Rachel yelled in the background.

My heart raced. "Are you at the estate?"

"Yes. I do apologize," he said in a hushed tone. "I thought that rather than reply to your email, I would surprise you at the estate. Not the best idea, it appears."

"What are you doing in Scotland?" Rachel had apparently snatched Nigel's phone. "You didn't leave Declan, did you?"

"Of course not. I told you I don't have cold feet."

She let out a relieved sigh.

"And get a grip. Don't scare Nigel off before he's even started."

"Sorry. Was just surprised to hear you're in Scotland. You left here without even saying goodbye so you could get home to Declan and Mac, and instead you went to Scotland?"

I explained my new job.

"Oh." She sounded hurt. "Congratulations. Can't believe you didn't call and tell me about a new job."

"I thought you might think I was ditching you, and I'm not. The job is part time, so I can still pop over on weekends for the weddings in October. I'll help get you through that crunch."

"I'm happy for you, seriously. Just wished you'd told me."

Feeling bad for not having confided in Rachel, I told her about the hat and Mrs. Muir. I left out the details about the hatbox stalkers on the plane and at her home.

"Someone tried to kill the woman?"

"The detective doesn't think it was attempted murder. Still waiting to hear, but he thinks she had a heart attack."

"You need to get out of there."

"I've already been through this with Declan. I'm on the first train and plane home in the morning. Don't worry. That woman is long gone. She was either after the hat or the paperwork. Regardless, she now has both."

"Are you sure you can trust this Winnie person?"

"She's legit. Michael recommended her. What would her motive be for having me deliver a hat so she could then have someone steal it? If she'd wanted it, she could have kept it rather than handing it over to me. And she has copies of the paperwork. Except for maybe the letter."

"Don't be trying to solve the mystery. Look what happened the last time. You discovered Cousin Enid is related to us!"

"I also solved the mystery of the missing macarons in Prague, with a thief involved in corporate espionage and other thefts." It had been more dumb luck and to save my ass.

"You can't compare finding a box of stolen cookies to finding a potential killer and thief who knows your identity."

"That waiter knew I was onto him. And don't forget—I wrote the script for the art mystery events at the estate and that story *Kitty the Kat Thief* in school."

"That doesn't qualify you to solve a real mystery."

I'd had no intention of sticking around to solve the mystery until Rachel just put me on the defense, as if I wouldn't be capable of it. Yet I put my bravado in check rather than arguing.

"I'll be fine. I'm locked in my guest room over a busy pub. The owner lives right down the hall. That woman has no reason to come after me now."

"Except that you know what she looks like. And if that Mrs. Muir woman dies, her imposter could be charged with unintentional manslaughter if she broke into the house and caused the heart attack."

On that reassuring note, I promised to keep Rachel posted and said good night. Now I really wished I had my defense spray. I unpacked my can of hair spray and set it on the nightstand. I shoved a small dresser in front of my door, along with a desk chair and anything else not bolted down. It reminded me of the first time I'd stayed alone in a Dublin hotel, working Rachel's meeting nearly a year ago. I'd been afraid that my stalker ex might have followed me to Dublin. Same as then, I was overreacting, alone in a hotel room in a foreign country. Yet I slipped the door's security lock in place.

That older woman wasn't that dangerous, was she? But what about the guy impersonating the nephew? I could outrun her. I wasn't so sure about him. I'd once outrun a nasty little Chihuahua and scaled a tree trunk without any branches. My parents' neighbors still talked about it. Yet I couldn't climb the rope in gym class. I could be pretty motivated when my life depended on it.

Hopefully, it didn't depend on it now.

My long, lace-covered voluminous white gown was a bit warm for the gorgeous sunny day. Even the poufy satin sleeves allowed for little air circulation. A breeze whipped the veil across my face, and I blew the tulle from my mouth. As I turned toward my new husband, the veil blew up, covering my eyes. We shared our first kiss as a married couple. The taste of Grandma's maple nutmeg cookies filled my mouth. I swept the veil from my face. Rather than Declan's dreamy blue eyes, a pair of devious green ones stared back at me. The hatbox guy!

I bolted upright in bed. In total darkness, it took me a moment to remember I was in a guest room over a pub. The sound of my heavy breathing filled the air. My *Coffey's Dublin* green tee clung to my body, drenched in sweat. If I opened a window to let in a breeze, I might also be letting in the stalker guy. I went and reached around the pile of furniture and double-checked the lock on the door. Secured.

At least I knew what I *didn't* want my wedding dress to look like—Mom's gown in my nightmare. I'd worn it for Halloween one year and teased my hair back to the eighties and accessorized my costume with white lace gloves made famous by Madonna.

I needed to call Mom.

It was 9:00 p.m. in Milwaukee. Hearing her voice would calm my racing heart. And I needed to check in. Not calling or shooting me daily wedding emails was unlike her. I'd have expected my mom to have had it planned by now.

"Oh hi, honey. I've been meaning to call and see if you've decided on a wedding date." Her upbeat voice was a warm welcome.

"I don't know yet." My tone held an edge of annoyance. "Sorry. Rachel has been on me about a date. I'll make a decision soon."

"Well, I'm guessing it won't be in January."

Not unless we eloped to the Caribbean.

"No. I don't picture a winter wedding."

Yay! Maybe by eliminating everything I *didn't* want, I'd narrow down what I *did* want.

"Good. Because I booked a singles cruise."

So much for calming my racing heart!

"Are you and dad getting divorced?"

"That's the same thing he asked me."

"I wonder why."

"No, we aren't getting divorced. I want to travel. He doesn't. I refuse to spend my retirement years vacationing in Green Bay and going to Packer football games because he doesn't care to travel. He claims it's because of his bad back, but he's flying nine hours to England for your wedding."

Yeah, he might not be, since my wedding likely wouldn't be in England! Before my travels began a year ago, my parents had only gone on one major trip—to Hawaii.

"But a singles cruise?"

"You act like I'm taking it to hook up with a man."

"I think that's what a lot of *men* might think."

"Believe me, I'm done caring about or trying to figure out what men are thinking and why. This cruise is for singles and solo travelers. There won't be a bunch of couples seated at dinner together, me the odd woman out. They have cocktail receptions, mixers, and activities geared toward your interests so you can meet others you have things in common with. Would be nice to find a future travel partner."

"What about Teri and Dottie?"

"My sisters said your wedding is the only trip they can make right now, due to finances. Yet Teri owns a crazy-expensive convertible she can only drive four months a year in Wisconsin, and Dottie drops a fortune at the spa monthly. Besides, I want to meet new people."

"Ah, okay. I hope Dad comes around."

"I told him either I travel, or we sell the house and move to Ireland."

Please travel! I loved my mom, but it was nice having a quality visit every few months. And I couldn't imagine my parents selling the ranch house I'd grown up in.

"When we come to Ireland or England or wherever you decide to get married, I'm going to stay in Ireland for a few weeks without your father. Don't worry—not going to ruin your honeymoon period. I'm going to get lost."

"What if I can't find you?"

Mom laughed. "That's what the tour is called. You get off the beaten path and have an adventure."

My mom was one of the least adventurous people I'd ever known.

"After I returned home from George and Fanny's wedding in England, I cried for days. I'm so glad you're getting married and making a home in Ireland and Rachel is working at the estate in England. But everyone is moving forward besides me, and of course your father because he's happy with his same daily routine. I'm not. I'm in a rut, and I need to get out of it."

Wow. Go Mom! Finally, Mom had faith in my ability to take care of myself, so she could now focus on herself. I would always need the comfort of knowing my mom was only a phone call away. Hopefully, my next call wasn't after another horrific nightmare about my wedding or the stalker dude.

Seven

ON THE TWO-HOUR train ride from Kilstruther to Edinburgh, Detective Orr phoned to confirm that Mrs. Muir had survived an eight-hour triple-bypass surgery. She was in critical condition and recovering in intensive care. Based on the timing, his theory was that prior to my arrival, the mystery woman broke into the house and gave Patricia a heart attack. I tried not to think about the fact that poor woman had been lying on the floor when I'd been feet away in the foyer. He also confirmed that her daughter was on her way from Australia and he'd be warning her to watch her back.

I left Winnie another message to report in on Mrs. Muir's condition and tell her about the man impersonating the woman's nephew. Also, I was anxious to know if Mr. Buckley had given her the okay to share information. She'd surely contact me the minute he did. I needed to back off. That was my last message, or she'd fire me for being annoying.

After no one had broken into my room overnight or

stalked me on the train, my sense of security and adventure had returned. Leaving the tram station to explore the city had been tempting. Declan wouldn't know I hadn't kept my promise, but I'd know. I headed straight to the airport—looking over my shoulder a few times to find nobody lurking in the shadows.

I zipped through check-in and security and headed toward my gate with a double-bagged tea and a croissant. Scotland T-shirts and souvenirs displayed in a shop window lured me inside. I snagged a box of the country's famous shortbread cookies, then perused clan pins in tartan patterns. Shaw. My surname was Scottish and had a tartan? I'd thought the name was English. I snatched the blue-and-green plaid kilt pin from the display. So much for no touristy trinkets. However, this was genealogy related. It might one day be a family heirloom. Walking past a magazine rack, I grabbed one with a smiling bride on the front cover. I checked out and attached the pin next to the Coffey pin on my pink purse strap.

While waiting to board at the gate, I searched out the Shaw surname online. It made the Top 100 Most Common Surnames in Scotland. Who knew? Clan Shaw once held a castle south of Inverness in the Scottish Highlands. A castle? Being a genealogist, I should have known the origin of my family surnames. Here I was in Scotland, the Shaws' homeland, and I hadn't a clue. I felt bad for having neglected my paternal family name.

I'd have to neglect it a bit longer, as I had no time to go off searching another family line right now. And certainly not alone in Scotland.

The scent of vanilla filled my head.

Heart racing, my gaze darted over my shoulder to a gentleman sitting behind me, head down, reading a magazine. He had short dark hair, and the hat on the seat next to him reminded me of the maple nutmeg cookie guy. My breathing quickened. He reached for the steaming beverage next to him and took a drink. It wasn't him. Merely a man drinking a vanilla latte. I let out a relieved woosh of air. However, I hadn't mistaken the scent of a fancy latte at the airport yesterday for the fake nephew. It'd been the exact same scent here and outside Mrs. Muir's house. Without a doubt.

My phone dinged the arrival of a text. I jumped, spilling tea down the front of my white lace blouse. Lovely.

Declan.

The emerald is real.

Declan met me at the Dublin airport and escorted me to my car in the parking ramp. I insisted on following him, since I'd be a nervous wreck with him behind me. I'd be analyzing my driving more than he would. A good thing I hadn't led the way, because I'd have missed several turns. My mind was focused on Mac having pooped out a real emerald. And that I'd been responsible for what was likely a several-million-euro stolen hat! That must have been the confidential information that Winnie had been wanting to share with me. The jeweler had recommended a gemologist in Dublin who could give a more accurate appraisal of an unset stone the size of a penny. According to him, a very high-quality emerald, sapphire, or ruby could be even more valuable per carat than a diamond.

We pulled onto Winnie's blacktop drive and parked to the side of the woman's cute little yellow car. The white bungalow with teal-trimmed windows appeared dark inside. After ringing the doorbell several times and nearly breaking a finger while pounding a fist against the solid wood door, I went and squinted through an open sliver in the drapes. The contents of the desk drawers were dumped on the floor, and the purple velvet chair lay on its side. Stuffing from the colorful beaded pillows trailed across the furnishings and hardwood floor. Winnie's feet in teal sandals stuck out from behind the couch.

"Winnie's on the floor!" I pounded on the window, hoping she wasn't unconscious and could hear me. My mind flashed back to imagine Patricia Muir lying on the floor after her massive heart attack.

We raced around back. Declan jimmied open a conservatory window using a flat-nosed garden hoe. We scuttled through the window and inside. Winnie lay sprawled on the floor, facedown. Her necklace's chunky stone pendant was next to her, and beads had scattered as far across the floor as her desk. I slapped a hand over my mouth in horror while Declan checked for a pulse.

"She's alive," he said.

In relief I collapsed onto the floor next to the woman. While Declan called for help, I gave her a pep talk that she was Windiana Jones and she'd be fine. After all the adventures she'd survived, she'd make it through this one too. Had Winnie been knocked out or suffered a heart attack like Mrs. Muir? My breathing quickened as I peered around at Winnie's lifetime collection of treasures now broken, shattered, and violated. The Charles Bridge painting had apparently been sent flying like a frisbee facedown across the scarred wood floor, sanding down the bright colors.

Anger-fueled adrenaline had me on my feet, determined to restore some semblance of order before Winnie returned home.

She *would* be returning home.

I hung the painting on the wall. I picked up a beaded teal pillow from India and started cramming the stuffing back inside.

"Best not be touching anything," Declan said. "This is a crime scene."

I dropped the pillow onto the floor. "Right. I wonder if Winnie walked in on an intruder tossing her house and the person came up from behind and knocked her out, or there was a scuffle and Winnie fought for her life. Either way the heartless horrible person left her lying there to die, same as Mrs. Muir. However, someone had called for help in Scotland. This has to be connected to the hat."

Declan shrugged. "Who knows. The woman might be mixed up with all sorts of dodgy characters. You've only known her a few days. And now you're involved in whatever this is."

"Michael wouldn't have recommended the job if Winnie was sketchy." I glanced at her empty desktop. "Her laptop is gone. It was sitting on her desk the other day. What was the person looking for? Something he'd assumed would be in with the hat's paperwork and wasn't? Like insurance and authenticity papers, since it appears the jewels are real? Or maybe the mystery woman ran off with the hat and now the couple thinks Winnie has it. If that were it, they'd have been following me yesterday to see if I was traveling with the hatbox. At least I hadn't led them to her. They'd already found her."

"And if they found Winnie, they could certainly find you."

Panic rushed through me. "Mac's home alone!"

Declan shook his head. "I dropped him off at Carter's pub to hang out with their dog since I knew we might be a bit."

I hugged Declan tightly. "Thank you."

"You should go hide out at George's estate until this is figured out."

"I'm not endangering everyone else. Besides, it's unlikely anyone is after me. I gave the woman everything I had except for the paperwork with her illegible signature, which is no clue. I was just hired two days ago. What's the chance anyone knows I work for Winnie, let alone my name?"

Had I told Patricia's impersonator merely my first name or also my last? I had an American accent. Not like she could have pegged me as an American living in Ireland unless she was in cahoots with the hatbox couple who were on my Dublin flight.

"If they'd known about me before my trip, they'd likely have stolen the hat from the house. Right?"

My phone dinged the arrival of a text. Hat photos from Zoe. Potential wedding hats were the last thing I felt like looking at right now!

The sound of approaching sirens made my heart race even faster. I had to find the person who did this before they found me!

Fifteen minutes later Winnie was being whisked away in an ambulance. I phoned Michael so he could be waiting for her at the hospital. Declan and I stayed behind to provide Garda Sweeney what information we had. I recounted my misadventures in Scotland and sent him photos of the three sketches.

"This has to be related to what happened in Scotland," I said. "Winnie thought there was something more to all this besides just the hat. The hat that turned out to have real jewels on it." I gasped. "Maybe the thief realized a jewel was missing from the hat and now she's looking for it. That's why the place was tossed. And it's my fault because Mac swallowed the emerald." My gaze darted to Declan. "That's it— he's off to doggy boarding school, and if they can't whip him into shape, then a doggy military academy."

Declan placed a hand on my arm. "I don't be thinking there's a doggy military academy, at least not in Ireland."

"Did the jeweler give you an estimate on the stone's value?" the officer asked.

Declan shrugged. "Said it could be anywhere from fifteen thousand to a hundred thousand euros, depending on the quality. Recommended I take it to a gemologist in Dublin."

"I'll actually be taking it." Garda Sweeney held out his hand.

Declan slipped the tissue-wrapped stone from his back pocket and handed it to the man, who in turn gave it to the other officer to bag as evidence. I gave him the contact info for Detective Orr in Scotland.

"You've only been employed by Ms. Dunne for two days?" he asked.

I nodded. "Correct.

"Where did you work before this?"

"I was an event planner at an estate in England."

"But you live in Ireland?"

I nodded.

His gaze narrowed on me. "How long have you been traveling back and forth between the two countries?"

I shrugged. "Since St. Patrick's Day. Once I took my dog, Mac, with me so I wouldn't be so lonely."

He quirked a suspicious brow. "The dog that swallowed the emerald?"

"Yep."

"Are ya saying she's a smuggler, and Mac's her jewel mule?" Declan said.

"What?" I screeched in horror. "No way would I ever intentionally have Mac swallow an emerald. What kind of a mother do you think I am? And of course I'd never knowingly transport jewels illegally. I worked at the Daly estate in Lancashire, where *Sunnyvale* filmed the wedding episode at the end of the season." I suddenly relied on the soap opera to give me credibility?

The other garda perked up. "Were you there when the wedding took place?"

I smiled. "It was quite lovely."

"Garda Whalen." Her boss gave her a stern look, and she got back to work.

"I guarantee neither Winnie nor I knew the jewels were real." Unless that was what she was planning to tell me. Not to confess that she'd been smuggling them, of course, or rather had *me* smuggling them. Maybe Clara O'Shea had been trying to get around Patricia Muir having to pay inheritance tax. I assumed the UK taxed such items, and it would be a boatload for a few-million-euro hat. "There were no authenticity papers or proof of insurance. The client estimated the value at five hundred euros."

"Do you have the contact information for your client, Mr. Fintan Buckley?"

"I have his company name." I slipped the confirmation of receipt from the envelope in my purse and gave him the company info. I needed to call Mr. Buckley and tell him about Winnie and warn him to watch his back.

If it wasn't already too late.

Eight

I LEFT Mr. Buckley a message about Winnie and warned him to be careful. He must have known the jewels were real. Clara O'Shea would have entrusted him with that key piece of information if she was relying on him to transport expensive jewels to Patricia Muir.

We found Michael pacing the green-carpeted waiting room. All he knew was that Winnie was in intensive care and they were running tests for head trauma and other injuries.

I brought him up to speed on the drama of the past two days and how I was certain the break-in at Winnie's had to be connected.

Michael steadied himself against his cane. "That's bloody awful. Yet I must say I'm thankful you were on the job. If you hadn't had the foresight to go and see her, she might not have been found in time."

I told him about Mac swallowing the jewel and that it was possibly my fault that the thief destroyed Winnie's house searching for it.

"That's nonsense, luv. You had no control over any of

this. How can't the two incidents be connected? Would be awfully coincidental."

"I'm wondering if Mr. Buckley claimed the hat was of little value to skirt inheritance taxes, and the handwritten letter may have explained this to Mrs. Muir."

"How was she related to Clara O'Shea?"

I shook my head. "Haven't a clue."

"If she was so distant a relation that they had to hire Winnie to locate her, then the estate and business must have been divided between the rest of the heirs. The O'Sheas were a wealthy family, at least at one point. It happens quite often that a family member moves to the UK and loses touch. We need to find Winnie's research and determine the other heirs."

"The hatbox couple without a doubt followed me from Ireland to Scotland. They had Irish accents. Could be relations of Clara O'Shea. If Winnie's research lists other relations, I could look online and try to find pictures of them and see if they match any of the three sketches."

"Unless, of course, the rellies didn't wish to do their own dirty work and hired the three people to do it for them," Declan said.

"Who else besides Mr. Buckley, Winnie, me, and possibly Clara O'Shea's relations would know when the hatbox was being delivered? Patricia Muir told her friend Gracie, the sketch artist, about the hat. Maybe she told others and exaggerated what she thought was the hat's value."

I dreaded having to tell the snarky Detective Orr he was right and the hat was valuable like he'd insisted.

"I'm not sure how we're going to find Winnie's research. Her laptop was stolen. Mr. Buckley would likely have a copy of the family history and, with any luck, the letter. When he returns my phone call, I can ask to see them."

"Winnie hid her laptop whenever she wasn't working on it," Michael said. "Perhaps it's tucked away in a secure location. I might know how to find it." He shook his head in disbelief. "Guess she'd been right to be so paranoid."

A doctor approached, and we stood at attention.

"We're waiting for the test results," he said. "She's in critical care. It's too soon to tell, but she's resting peacefully. There was blood found on her stone necklace. It wasn't responsible for her head injury. She must have hit her attacker with it. The forensic team swabbed it for DNA. The results will take a bit and will depend on what DNA is in the database to compare it against. You're best off being on the lookout for someone with an injury."

If the person's DNA wasn't in the database, we'd need evidence, motive, and probable cause to have a warrant to obtain it from a suspect, if we found one. At least that was how it always went on TV shows.

Michael smiled for the first time since we'd arrived at the hospital. "That's my Winnie. Always thinking, leaving behind a DNA clue to solve the mystery if she's...not able to." He fought back tears.

I slipped a comforting arm around his shoulders. "She'll be able to tell us what happened."

The thief had left DNA at the crime scene. Did that mean he was a rookie, injured too badly to think clearly, or was interrupted and had to bolt before he could grab the evidence with his DNA?

I wanted justice. If he hurt Winnie while looking for the stupid jewel Mac had swallowed, I'd never forgive myself.

Whoever had left Winnie on the floor to die and destroyed her lifetime collection of memories was going down!

Blue-and-white crime scene tape cordoned off Winnie's door. Michael pulled back the corner of the mat on the front stoop.

"She keeps a key under the doormat?" I shot a nervous glance over my shoulder, making sure the garda or thief weren't watching us. "That's the first place someone would look."

Michael smiled. "Precisely why the key isn't there. Merely a clue to its location." He pointed out a tiny plastic ladybug.

"Right, then," Declan said. "How's that a clue?"

We followed Michael out back to a fairy house with a large ladybug on the side. He peeked inside the house and removed a weathered seed package for tomatoes. He was off to the greenhouse, where he dug through potted tomato plants until he uncovered a key.

"She switches the hiding spot regularly, making it a bit of a treasure hunt. Winnie loves a good mystery." He gave me a wink.

We entered the house through the back conservatory. Michael placed a hand to his chest, peering in horror at Winnie's damaged belongings. Beads from her stone necklace lay scattered across the floor. A haze of tears filled his eyes, then anger darkened his gaze. He picked up a colorful embroidered picture frame, the glass front shattered. It displayed a photo of Winnie holding a monkey, wooden boats floating in a canal behind her.

"The floating markets in Thailand." He smiled faintly. "I'd have been worried about contracting some rare disease, whereas Winnie welcomed the little furry creature with open arms."

"We probably shouldn't be touching anything," Declan said. "Also, should be getting out in case the thief returns. Once the crime scene tape is removed, we'll get the place back in shape before Winnie is home from the hospital."

"And she *will* be returning home," I said.

Michael placed the photo frame back on the floor next to a vibrant red-and-blue painting with boats sailing on a river. "That's the Bosporus in Istanbul. She could never replace that piece of artwork."

Declan placed a reassuring hand on Michael's shoulder. "I'll be able to repair the damage. I promise."

Michael nodded. "Best be finding that laptop so we can find whoever did this and make them pay."

He marched into the kitchen and opened a cupboard. He reached back into a cubby in the exposed stone wall. No laptop. Snatching a key from a hook in the conservatory, he was off to the woodshed. He removed an empty box of plant food from a shelf and slipped out a hard-sided laptop case.

A celebratory smile spread across his face. He removed the computer and turned it on. The page requested a passcode.

"Try WinifredDunne1941."

I typed it in, and the computer rejected it.

"WindianaJones1941."

Nope.

"Constantinople1941. That's where she was born. When her father was transferred there for work. Of course, it was renamed Istanbul by that time, but she still called it by what she felt was its given name, not its nickname. And she was given the middle name Constance based on her birthplace."

Nada.

"Try it with an exclamation mark at the end."

Yes! We'd accessed Winnie's computer.

"We best be leaving," Michael said. "Please keep me posted on what you find or should you be needing assistance navigating her filing system. If I recall correctly, it's much more straightforward than locating the house key."

I nodded. "I have a better shot at figuring out any clues on the computer than the garda do. And technically it wasn't left 'at' the scene of the crime."

Declan quirked a questioning brow.

"We didn't have to cut through any crime tape to get into the woodshed, did we?"

Michael agreed with a sharp nod. "Most certainly did not."

Declan held his hands up in defeat.

"Please promise that whatever clues you find on Winnie's computer you'll turn over to the garda and not investigate yourself." Declan glanced at me from the driver's seat. He'd insisted I was too frazzled to drive and had me leave my car at the hospital.

I nodded.

"I mean it. Please don't get any further involved in all of this. These people are dangerous. This isn't a Windiana Jones adventure—this is serious. You're not a detective."

"A genealogist *is* a detective," I quipped.

"Seriously, Caity."

"If these people think I have what they want, they'd already be looking for me regardless if I investigate what happened to Winnie. Besides, this might all be my fault because of that stupid emerald."

A siren wailed in the distance.

Declan and I exchanged panicked glances.

It grew louder as we approached the bend before our house.

Our security alarm!

"It appears they may have found you."

My heart went berserk. Thankfully, Mac was safe and sound at Carter's pub. He could have been kidnapped and held for ransom until I produced whatever it was this person wanted.

At the end of our tree-lined drive sat a garda vehicle. Relief washed over me, until I realized the two officers had apprehended the intruder—my sister.

"What the hell?" I flew from the car.

Rachel grimaced, pressing her hands over her ears. "Tell this officer I'm your sister," she shouted over the siren.

I confirmed her identity with the officer while Declan raced inside and deactivated the alarm. Cows mooed loudly in the distance, protesting the high-pitched noise. The officers left, and Declan headed over to Carter's pub to pick up Mac. Relief washed over me again that Mac hadn't been home, even though Rachel had turned out to be the intruder. What if it hadn't been her?

Rachel dropped onto the front steps and frantically rifled through her carry-on bag, sucking in deep, rapid breaths, like she was in labor. She pulled out a blood pressure monitor. After securing the cuff around the top of her arm, she closed her eyes and pressed the button. The monitor hummed to life and beeped moments later.

Rachel checked the results. She let out a distressed squeak. "I have to relax." More deep breathing.

"What are you doing here?"

"When you mentioned you were in Scotland, I thought that's what I need to do. Get away for a few days."

"So why aren't you in *Scotland*? It's only a few hours by train and not the eight hours to get here. And you don't have time to get away for a few days."

"I'm not capable of setting boundaries as a planner." She shook her head vigorously. "I thought quitting Brecker and all the traveling would reduce my stress. I mean, what could be less stressful than living on a quiet English estate? But it's not quiet. If I don't get effin' peace and quiet soon, I'm going to end up with kidney failure or a stroke. This job could be the death of me."

"*Every* job will be the death of you unless you learn to manage your stress. You were always an overachiever. Now it's time to achieve a balanced lifestyle. You need to talk to your therapist."

"I don't have one."

"Precisely. You need to get one."

"You're the one who sucked me into becoming the estate's planner and then deserted me."

I stabbed a thumb to my chest. "Me?"

"The art mystery events were your idea to get the estate back on its feet."

"You took it to a whole other level, booking too many

teas and weddings." I took a calming breath. "If you need a short break, go into Dublin and stay with Gerry. You moved in there. I'm sorry. This is really bad timing. I have a lot going on."

Not wanting her blood pressure monitor to explode, I decided not to tell her anything more than she already knew about Mrs. Muir in the ER and the stolen hat.

Rachel fought back tears. "I might have messed things up with Gerry. He went back to the pub."

Who the hell *was* at the estate? I certainly wasn't going back there!

I fought the urge to grab the monitor and check my own blood pressure. However, I hadn't a clue what my normal pressure was.

"For starters, get on some antianxiety meds," I said.

I was seriously considering it myself.

Rachel nodded.

"Did Gretchen totally freak out about you leaving? *She* didn't leave, did she?"

"She doesn't know I'm gone. I told her I had an appointment this morning."

"An *eight*-hour appt?"

"I left at five a.m. I should probably call her."

"I'll give her a ring and make sure she knows you're okay and beg her not to quit when she finds out she's in charge." I stepped away and phoned Gretchen to apologize for this madness that she hadn't signed up for.

"I think it's best she stays there for a bit," Gretchen said. "Everyone could use a break from her. Even me, and I just got here three days ago."

Blood raced through my veins, causing my temples to pulsate. "I thought she'd backed off and was doing better?"

"Oh, she has. That's the problem. She bought a blood pressure monitor and checks her bp a half dozen times a day. If she feels it's too high, she sits on a bench and stares at the *Venus de Milo* and *David* shrubs as if she's in a Paris art museum admiring the original statues. She's right where everyone parks. Several people have come in worried that a woman on a bench out front had a stroke. Then I panic, since my coworker just had a massive one, and I race outside to check on her. It's best for both of us if she takes a few days off."

What about what was best for *me*?

Rachel was staring at the purple hydrangea bush, the blood pressure device dangling at her side. Her eerily calm, comatose state was more concerning than her manic planner mode.

"Nigel is looking for a reason to escape his crazy aunt, so he agreed to return today and fill in for her."

The estate was becoming a meeting planners' rehab center. I'd already done my time in that rehab.

I repeat, I was *not* returning to the estate.

"Harriet and Dot from Fanny's bridge club are going to help out. I'm fine, Caity. Seriously. It'll be good for Rachel to get away for a few days. It'll be good for all of us."

As long as a few days didn't turn into a few weeks.

I promised to keep Gretchen posted.

I settled Rachel in the guest room, then led her out back to relax on a lounge chair in the fairy garden, with a steaming mug of chamomile tea.

Declan and Mac returned from the pub.

I dropped to my knees and smothered Mac in kisses. "Mommy was just upset. She'd never, ever send you to doggy boarding school or military academy. You're staying right here with Mommy and Daddy forever."

Mac nuzzled his wet nose against my cheek.

"Rachel's sitting out in the garden staring at the tiny fairy door on the tree," Declan said. "Like she's wondering what's behind the door but doesn't have the energy to open it and find out. I asked how she was getting on, and she gave me a faint nod."

"I know. Her calmness is more concerning than her meltdowns. She's officially put on an around-the-clock watch starting now." I smiled down at Mac. "Since you're the only one without a crazy life at the moment, you're in charge of Rachel."

Mac's tail went wild, slapping against the kitchen cupboard. Glad somebody was up to the challenge.

Nine

FIFTEEN MINUTES later I had two fluffy pillows propped up against the bed's headboard behind my back. Three teabags floated in a steaming cup of water. Three should be enough caffeine. Thankfully, Winnie's computer filing system wasn't a convoluted treasure hunt that took me all day to find Patricia's file. The file contained three documents: Contract, Family History, and Notes. No Aunt Clara's Letter.

I tapped a finger against the keyboard. A contract was confidential, yet wasn't confidentiality out the window when Winnie was in the ER fighting for her life? I clicked it open. Winnie made an hourly rate of a hundred euros. Wow. No wonder the woman could afford all those exotic travels. I skimmed through the legalese to Winnie's role outlined in detail.

To locate Eleanor O'Shea's biological daughter, heir to the O'Shea Estate in County Galway...

Who was *Eleanor* O'Shea? Was her daughter Patricia heir

to an *estate*, not merely the lovely magenta-and-lime-green gemstone hat?

Winnie's ethical dilemma might not have been over whether or not to tell me about the jewels being real but whether to divulge Patricia's true identity and full inheritance. Yet someone stealing the letter and hat wouldn't keep Patricia from learning the truth. Mr. Buckley and Winnie could merely forward another letter...

Or couldn't they, if they were both dead?

Goose bumps raced up my back and down my arms.

If Patricia were dead, her inheritance would go to her daughter rather than any distant O'Shea relations. Rellies who might have used scare tactics or other means to induce a heart attack to make it appear the woman died of natural causes.

I opened the Family History document and skimmed through three pages of background. Clara and Eleanor's father had acquired his wealth as a hotelier. He was partners with a hotel baron until the 1950s, when the two men had a falling-out. Mr. O'Shea sold his shares in a famous Kerry resort and created a successful business renting holiday cottages. The family owned a lovely 350-acre estate in Galway, which was now Patricia's.

Her mother, Eleanor, had been a schoolteacher. Aww... That would make Patricia happy. Eleanor had studied education at the University of St. Andrews. She was an established cellist who often played with the Dublin symphony, until she moved to a cottage in Donegal for a teaching position. She never married. Her only sibling, Clara was an artist and remained on the O'Shea estate until her recent death. Their mother had lived with Clara until the mom had died at ninety-eight. Winnie was a great storyteller, not merely detailing dry facts.

Four living relations were mentioned, along with contact information. One was the daughter of Clara's first cousin, and the rest were second cousins, sharing great-grandparents in common with Clara. The first cousin's daughter lived on the O'Shea estate. Well, that was interesting. Fearing she'd be kicked out if Patricia inherited the estate would have been motive for attempted murder.

Eleanor's only child was Patricia, and Clara never had children. Curious if the impostors were distant relations, I searched online for their photos but didn't find much. Not even on social media. I could take a road trip to County Galway to pay my condolences. See if one of them happened to have a large gash on their head from Winnie's deadly stone necklace.

The relations must have known about Patricia's true identity if they were guilty. Or maybe they knew Patricia was inheriting the hat but didn't know her family connection. Distant relations would inherit much less than Eleanor's daughter, unless Patricia were dead. Definite motive for attempted murder. Yet the next heir in line would be Eleanor's granddaughter. They wouldn't need to off her for the hat they already had, but they might for the estate. Detective Orr had already warned Patricia's daughter to watch her back, but I should inform him that the stakes were just raised.

Winnie's family history report didn't mention the hat's value or its family significance. Aunt Clara's handwritten letter likely provided an explanation. In that case neither Winnie nor Mr. Buckley had likely known the hat's value unless they'd read the letter before the envelope was sealed. I was worried that I still hadn't heard from Mr. Buckley. You'd think he'd at least call me back to check on Winnie's condition.

Based on Eleanor's child's original birth certificate, Patricia's dad's name was John Kelly. No information was provided for him. Even the amazing Winnie would have difficulty sorting through hundreds, if not thousands, of Irish men with one of the most common first and last names in the country.

The Notes document contained the scanned birth record and newspaper clippings about Mr. O'Shea's success and unfortunate failure in the hotel industry. How his flagship property was bought out by the Moran Corporation. Headlines mainly focused on business dealings, with a few about his wife's charitable contributions and involvement in local organizations. The birth record noted the baby's name as Patricia Mildred. Interesting that the adoptive parents kept at least the child's first name.

I went down to the peach room, where Declan was lying on the couch, feet up, paging through my bridal magazine. At least I assumed it was mine and that he hadn't bought his own copy.

"Taking a break. Limiting myself to two paintings a day. Don't want to end up sitting out in the garden next to Rachel, staring at fairies."

I nodded. "Good idea."

"Hope you don't mind. Saw this sticking out of your carry-on bag. These dresses are fierce expensive."

"They're what I call inspiration dresses. To give you an

idea of what you want in a wedding gown so you can have it custom made for less or search for a similar cheaper one."

"Which one do you fancy?"

No clue since I hadn't opened the magazine.

"This one here looks similar to Shauna's." His gaze darted to mine. "Sorry. Probably shouldn't be talking about my first wedding."

"Yes, you should." Declan rarely discussed Shauna. I took advantage of any chance I could to get him to open up about her. He moved his feet, and I sat next to him, glancing over at the magazine. The long satin dress had pearl buttons up the back. "That's gorgeous. Elegant and traditional."

He nodded. "She wanted traditional. We were married in the Killybog church. Big bouquets of yellow flowers deco-rated the end of each pew. My tie was yellow, her favorite color."

"That sounds lovely."

"Then we went to my mate Peter Molloy's pub for the reception. Also traditional, since weddings took place in pubs back generations. The gathering place of the community."

"Should we get married in the Killybog church?"

Grandma hadn't been married at the old stone Catholic church. Being estranged from their families, she and her husband had married at a Protestant church in England.

"Oh wait." I smiled. "Were you kicked out of the church before or after your wedding?"

"A few years before, and the priest still allowed us to marry there. And in all fairness to me, that fella was looking for a fight. And I was in the right." He turned his attention back to the magazine. "So which dress inspires you?"

"That's a secret. You can't see my dress until the day of the wedding. It's bad luck." And a great excuse not to show him a dress I hadn't yet picked out. However, that 1920s-style wedding dress in the photo at Patricia Muir's had caught my eye. "I plan to go dress shopping soon. Will ask Fanny, Rachel, your mom, and Zoe to go along. Will make a girls' day out of it."

When would Rachel and I have time for a girls' day?

I shared my findings about Eleanor O'Shea having been Patricia Muir's biological mother.

He raised an intrigued brow. "So her inheritance went from a lovely jeweled hat to an entire estate? That certainly gives people motive for attempted murder, not merely theft."

"I know. I'm worried about Winnie. If these people didn't find what they were looking for at her house, likely the laptop or the emerald, maybe they're lurking around the hospital waiting for her to wake up so they can question her and then..." I bit down on my lower lip.

Declan's gaze narrowed. "Have the feeling you're going to pay Mr. Buckley a visit with or without me, so I'm going with ya. It's odd the fella isn't returning your calls."

I nodded. "I'm curious if he has a copy of the aunt's letter. I need to read that letter."

I'd tell Declan about wanting to pay the O'Shea relations a visit later, to see if they were the people in the unidentified sketches. One step at a time.

"I'll go with you to Mr. Buckley's office tomorrow."

God, I loved this man!

I flung my arms around Declan's neck and kissed him senseless. He smelled like freshly fallen rain and woodsy cologne. Declan curled his fingers into the back of my shirt and pressed my body against his. I let out a moan, then reluctantly drew back, peering into the lustful look in his dreamy blue eyes.

"Rachel's right outside." I glanced over my shoulder, making sure she wasn't standing in the doorway wearing that eerie calm look, watching *us* instead of the fairies. "I should check on her."

Declan dropped his head back and groaned in protest before giving me an agreeable kiss.

I went out to the fairy garden. No Rachel or Mac. A tiny purple door hung at the base of a massive oak's trunk. A sign on the door read, *Sshh. Fairies sleeping.* A whimsical metal teapot painted in vivid pinks, blues, and purples was decorated with ladybugs and flowers. A small purple fairy stood in a yellow teacup, her elbows resting on the cup's rim. Thanks to Mac and a weasel chasing each other, the teacup had flown through the air, the fairy decapitated. You could barely tell I'd glued her little head back on.

I went upstairs and peeked into the guest room in case Rachel had come inside without me hearing her. She hadn't. I went down to ask Declan if he'd seen her, when I spied her through the front window, by the Coffey cottage and dressed in a yellow vest with silver reflective stripes.

"She's not planning to take Mac for a walk, is she?"

I flew down the drive. Mac was lying on the ground, enjoying the sunshine. Rachel was peering inside the cottage through a glassless window, brushing a finger over the gnarly vines climbing up the side of the house. The plaster framing the window had crumbled away, revealing brick and jagged-edged stones. Inside, moss covered the faded whitewashed walls and large stone fireplace. Ivy dangled from the ceiling, and clumps of straw from the original thatched roof were tucked between the wooden-pegged beams.

"Imagine a family of seven having lived in this tiny house," Rachel said. "And we always thought our family's ranch with one bathroom was too small for us."

"Yeah, and when Grandma's sister Agnes died here in 1985, she still didn't have indoor plumbing or electricity."

"Maybe that's why kids were afraid of her."

I'd told Rachel the story a neighbor had shared about whenever he was naughty, his parents would say, "Ya better behave, or we'll drop you off at Agnes Coffey's."

"It's weird being on the same land Grandma hadn't stepped foot on since leaving Ireland for England and then America. I couldn't imagine never going back home for the holidays, to attend weddings and funerals, and just to visit."

Rachel had never been the type to reflect on the past, especially if it wasn't her past. She'd always been about living in the moment and the future.

Rachel smiled. "I'm glad you and Declan are here to watch over the place."

"Me too. This is one of the best decisions I've ever made."

Rachel continued staring inside the cottage.

"When the teas and weddings eventually slow down, we'll come up with other ideas," I said. "You're not in this alone. We're both pretty creative. Now that the estate is open to the public, we can seek funding from the government or a historical conservation group to maintain the upkeep. There are six bedrooms. Once the ceilings are repaired, we could turn it into a B and B. Fanny would love baking scones for a few couples rather than a few dozen people three times a day.

Or we could turn the place into a rehab facility for meeting planners."

Rachel wore an intrigued smile. "A great therapy session would be beating the hell out of an LCD projector. I hate setting up those things. And throwing darts at a crazy-ass client's photo."

"We could write therapeutic letters to our worst clients. Mine, of course, would be the Blair Bitch Project from my Prague meeting. That chick was a nightmare."

Rachel rattled off several ideas, becoming a bit too enthusiastic about opening a center for unhinged planners.

"Promise me you won't schedule any further events until we get everything under control."

Like you.

"I *can't* book any more. Every weekend is booked except one in December."

My jaw dropped. "I thought there were seven weddings before the end of the year, four of which were in October?"

Rachel shook her head.

My heart raced. "Cancel a few of them."

She looked at me like *I* was the one who'd gone off the deep end. "Are you crazy? The estate is under contract and could get sued." She grimaced. "What are we going to do?"

"Have you committed."

"I know, right?"

"I'm serious. If we can prove you weren't of sound mind when you signed the contracts, the estate is off the hook."

"Like hell I'm going into a psych ward so some judge can rule the contracts void. What happened to *we* can get through anything together?"

I took a deep breath. "Maybe my planner rehab idea

would work to void the contracts. Have all of us committed to the estate so no events can be held there." I was going to need to be committed somewhere...soon!

Rachel collapsed a shoulder against the window frame, and pieces of plaster crumbled to the ground. "I don't know what I was thinking. The money was just too tempting. And I was worried that after the whole *Sunnyvale* hype dies down there'll be no business. That I'd given everyone false hope. I've been freaking out not knowing how to admit what I've done. I didn't expect so much interest in weddings this fall. Thought we'd have time to get organized before spring wedding season."

"Seriously, who books their wedding venue only a month out?" It'd taken me six weeks to decide on the color for my bridesmaid dresses and to buy a bridal magazine to start thinking about my own dress.

"Several crazed fans canceled their booked venues and paid massive fees so they could book the estate. A few moved wedding dates up from next year. And one person got engaged last week and decided to marry in September. I've also never worked on the venue end of the industry so wasn't prepared for the insane number of phone calls and site inspections."

"Yeah, hasn't that one woman been there three times?"

"Four. Still, after the fourth one she called wondering what colors the flowers are in the garden. The purpose of the site inspection is to be taking photos of everything. If it's not brides, it's their planner or the photographer, caterer, décor company. Vendors want to see the place because they've never done an event there. I spend my days doing site inspections and chatting on the phone with brides-to-be or, even worse, with their mothers." She tossed her arms up in frustration, sending more plaster flying from the window frame.

I slipped a hand behind her back and eased her away from the house.

"Even brides with spring weddings are returning with the wedding party because they want to see where the soap opera was filmed. And then I had that batshit-crazy fan wanting to book the place for her dream wedding, which is still a dream because she doesn't even have a boyfriend!"

I nodded in understanding. When was Rachel supposed to have time to do the planning?

"Oh, and now some chick wants to see about swapping out Thomas's *Venus De Milo* and *David* shrubs with two Degas ballerina shrubs because she studied ballet in Paris. Thomas about had a stroke that time the sheep got lose and ate off David's private parts and he had to replace them with prosthetic ones. As if we're going to change out decade-old shrubs for that wacky chick. That was when I hopped the ferry over here!" She glanced around. "I need my bp monitor!"

"Relax..." I placed my hands on Rachel's shoulders and directed her toward the field across the road. "Look at the sheep along the ridge in the distance."

She took calming breaths, doing several neck rolls while peering out at the sheep.

"Take the wedding page off the estate's website at least until the hype dies down. Or say 'available for elopements only,' so you're merely dealing with the couple. If couples want to do a site inspection, then recommend booking an afternoon tea."

"Corporate meetings are much more cut and dry, with

one demanding CEO. I can see why most wedding planners only plan ten to fifteen weddings per year, not per *season*."

"First off, you need to delegate half the weddings to Gretchen. Nigel, George, and Fanny can tag team on the teas, which we will no longer hold on Sundays because we are not going to be up all night breaking down wedding setup and preparing for teas on Sundays. We'll be closed Sunday and Monday. Teas will be Tuesday through Friday, ending at two p.m. on Friday because brides are going to want access to decorate for the big day Saturday."

Rachel nodded, a faint smile curling her lips. "We'll be fine, right? It'll all work out?"

"We'll live through it."

However, I wasn't sure what shape we'd be in afterward.

Rather than picturing myself trekking across the Australian outback or cruising around Tuscany in a sporty red convertible, visions of the English estate housing a planner rehab facility took shape in my mind...

Ten

THE FOLLOWING MORNING, Declan and I were in our jammies relaxing on the couch in the peach room, enjoying our morning tea before heading out to see Mr. Buckley. Mac lay curled on the chair, soaking up the sunshine through the open drapes. Rachel walked into the room, her white cotton pajamas, hair, and skin covered in purple powder. Declan, Mac, and I all sniffed the air. Mac trotted over to Rachel, his nose going wild.

I breathed in the scent of lavender. "Is that lavender powder?"

"Lavender pixie dust. Sleeping powder."

Mac nuzzled his nose into Rachel's pant leg.

"Mac, sit!" I yelled.

He obeyed, still sniffing the air.

"Too much lavender is toxic for dogs. Did he sleep with you?"

"My friend's dog has an aroma bear stuffed animal made for pets. Each squeak releases calming lavender essential oils to help reduce his anxiety when she's at work during the day."

"I don't care what she has. I've read lavender items can be harmful to dogs, and you're doused in, like, a bottle of it. Stop using it here. And wash your sheets, or he'll be all over your bed."

"Gee, so much for waking up feeling relaxed and stress-free."

Still sitting, Mac craned his neck toward Rachel, sniffing.

I clapped my hands. "Mac, hop up." He reluctantly jumped back up onto the chair.

I glanced over at Declan. "We can't leave him here."

"Seriously?" Rachel sank onto a chair. "He'll be fine. I promise—no more lavender."

"No chocolate, coffee, or—"

"Are you talking about Mac or me? I can't function without my morning coffee." She flashed me a sarcastic grin. "I'm not going to feed Mac human food. Don't worry."

"All right, fine."

"You seem in better form than yesterday," Declan said.

"Thanks. I took Caity's advice on learning to manage my stress. My voicemail is full again after just cleaning it out two days ago. So instead of listening to a message then deleting it, I leave it. That way my voicemail message will tell callers that the box is full and please try again later."

"Yeah, that's not really what I meant by managing."

"And every time I respond to an email, the person shoots me another question. I'll wait until I get a half dozen emails from someone before responding so I can answer all the questions at once. Brilliant time management, don't you think?"

"Right, then," Declan said. "Doubt clients will be thinking that's so brill. They might be getting a wee bit angry if you haven't responded by their third or fourth email."

"That's even better. If they cancel their contract with the estate, *we* can't be sued." She snapped her fingers with a victorious grin. "Voila."

"Um, I think we need a better strategy," I said. "At least for future weddings. Like maybe increasing the rental fee. The whole work smarter, not harder concept."

"I think we need more tea." Declan stood, glancing over at Rachel. "And a coffee?"

She smiled. "Yes please."

"Okay, time for a game plan," I said. "Sort your emails into client folders and write down your voicemail messages. Don't delete them until tomorrow."

A distressed look wrinkled Rachel's forehead, and her breathing quickened.

"Select the clients that would be easiest to hand over to Gretchen. Organize the files, and review them with her."

"Do I have to review them in person?"

"It'd be a lot easier. And you can't avoid the estate for much longer."

Rachel slumped back in the green velvet chair.

"I'm sure George can handle site inspections once teas are down to four days a week and two daily. He can address questions and offer to pass along any he can't answer to you."

The wrinkles in Rachel's forehead relaxed. "You should be a meeting planner."

I shook my head. "Don't even go there."

"Just kidding." She walked over and gave me a hug. "Thanks for helping and for not kicking me out."

Kind of weird for me to be the one giving Rachel planning advice.

"Please don't tell anyone about my meltdown. I might lose my credibility. They might no longer see me as their fearless leader."

"That'll never happen."

"Do you think Ireland sells hotdogs? Remember how Mom sliced up hotdogs and heated them with baked beans when we were little?"

"Now serving that dish at a wedding might hurt your credibility. But it sounds delish. I think they have hotdogs here. If not, the convenience store sells a killer prepared mac and cheese."

We were both in need of comfort food.

On the way to the garda station, I called the hospital and checked on Winnie, who was still in stable condition. Thank God. I couldn't handle one more *un*stable person in my life right now.

Detective Orr reported that Patricia Muir was on the road to recovery and that her daughter had landed safely. I filled him in on Winnie's research and that Patricia was Eleanor O'Shea's biological daughter, heir to the O'Shea estate. Certainly a motive for relations to want to off the woman if they knew her identity.

Zoe texted. *Guess you didn't fancy my hat ideas?*

Crap. I hadn't even looked at them. I glanced at the photos. The hats weren't as flashy as the first ones but still a bit much.

Maybe I should skip the hat. I asked her to find a hat or fascinator similar to the red one Declan had given her. Small, worn off to the side of the head, with a few simple flowers or a piece of lace.

Fingers crossed that the third time was a charm, or Zoe might quit looking and I'd feel awful. Not to mention I didn't have time to look for my own hat when I was searching for a stolen one!

When we arrived at the station, I recounted my discovery and theory to Garda Sweeney.

"How exactly did you obtain Winnie Dunne's research since I last saw you?" he asked.

"Being an employee, I have access to the company computer. She sometimes stores it outside, or rather off site, so thankfully it wasn't at the crime scene." My palms started sweating. "I could forward you the files, but Winnie signed a confidentiality agreement, so I'm not sure if—"

"Well, *I'm* sure. Please forward me the files."

I smiled. "Will do. The O'Shea relations are a good lead, aren't they?"

"If one of them stole the hat, it happened on Scottish soil, not Irish."

"The two cases are connected."

"We don't know that for sure."

"Do you have any leads making you think they aren't related?"

"I'm not at liberty to discuss." He glanced down at the files on his desk.

"There's something you aren't telling us. And it certainly isn't evidence proving Mac and I are jewel smugglers, because we aren't. Yet despite you wrongly accusing us of the crime, I was gracious enough to come here and share what I'd uncovered."

"That's grand. Then I won't be accusing you of impeding an investigation."

Declan shot me a warning look to cool the snarkism.

"You seem busy," I said. "We should be going."

Declan and I headed out of the station.

"You're going to end up getting yourself arrested," Declan said.

"Why? I shared everything I learned about Patricia Muir's background and the hat. He should at least tell me if he has a lead to motivate me to share future information."

"Maybe he thinks you're feeding him false information to look less suspicious. Besides, staying out of jail for impeding an investigation should be motivation enough."

"It's not. I shouldn't have given him that info on Clara O'Shea's relations and their possible motive. Maybe he's lying about not following that lead, and if he contacts them before I get over to Galway, I've lost the element of surprise. They'd be chattier with me than that arrogant Garda Sweeney and more apt to slip up and tell me something they shouldn't."

Declan shot me a curious look. "Plan to go visit the rellies in Galway, do ya now?"

"I need to pay my condolences for the loss of their cousin Clara O'Shea."

"What about being worried about leaving Mac with Rachel?"

"We'll go tomorrow and take Mac with us. She'll be headed back to the estate."

If I had to put her on the ferry myself.

Eleven

I CALLED Mr. Buckley's office since I hadn't had luck reaching him on his cell phone. His assistant informed me that he was working out of his home today. Where that home was located, she wasn't at liberty to say. That response was getting irritating. Tracking down someone using people-search sites in Ireland wasn't as easy as in the US due to the EU's strict GDPR data protection and privacy laws. However, I found Mr. Fintan Buckley mentioned in an online church newsletter for a small village in County Wicklow, just south of Dublin. It was an hour drive from the Mullingar garda station, so we headed down to check on the lawyer. I popped into the local post office, pretending to be lost, asking for directions to Mr. Buckley's. I'd perfected the damsel-in-distress act from years of being one. The kind gentleman directed me to a large stone house down a narrow road a mile out of town.

Nobody answered the doorbell. Curtains covered the front windows, so we headed around back, finding slitted curtains. We peeked inside at the living room that didn't appear to have been ransacked by a thief. Yet it looked too disorganized for the meticulous lawyer. I couldn't imagine him allowing a picture frame to go un-straightened. Framed black-and-white photographs of trees hung crooked on the gray walls. Yet they *hung*.

"Why didn't the robber rip the photos out of the frames when tearing the place apart, like he did at Winnie's?" I asked.

"Better question, why didn't he nick the photos? Sean Murphy's photographs are worth loads. Several thousand euros each. There's, like, twenty-five thousand euros on those walls."

My top lip curled back. "For those?" Vases in various shades of gray were tipped over around the hearth of the gray marble fireplace. "Not one broken vase."

Declan nodded. "Looks a bit staged, doesn't it now? Winnie's looks like gale-force winds tore through it, whereas this looks more like a soft breeze blew through."

"Totally. And it's usually a guilty person who stages a crime scene to make himself look innocent. We should still go in just in case and make sure he's okay and not stuck under something heavy. Or is on his last breath and needs to tell me where to find a copy of Clara O'Shea's letter."

"No way. We'd had a key to Winnie's house. That wasn't breaking and entering. This would be. You're not getting arrested over this. Besides, his car isn't here. He's not stuck under a heavy object inside." He rang 999.

"Maybe the break-in wasn't staged. The thief was careful not to damage the valuable artwork because he planned to return for it. Maybe Mr. Buckley came home and the thief had to escape out the back. When the lawyer saw his house, he went to warn Winnie. That was two days ago. Where's he been, and why hasn't he reported the break-in? Unless he's been gone and hasn't returned to find his house broken into. Maybe he did get my message warning him to watch his back and hasn't come home. Now he's hiding out or running for his life. Regardless of which house was broken into first, I wonder if the person found what he was looking for at either place."

Fifteen minutes later the garda, rather than Declan and me, were breaking into Mr. Buckley's home. How had the intruder gotten in if the house was locked? And why wasn't the security system set, considering all the valuable photographs? The paramedics were on standby. However, Mr. Buckley wasn't in need of medical attention, at least not here. He was gone.

I explained to the officer how this had to be related to the break-in at Winnie's. And that she was in the hospital fighting for her life. I gave the garda pics of the three sketches and the contact info for the other two officers involved in what was becoming quite the international case. I didn't mention I'd discovered Mrs. Muir's real identity thanks to Winnie's research. I'd already given the tip about the rellies in Galway to Garda Sweeney and regretted potentially losing the element of surprise when I popped over to visit them. Besides, the three police forces should be sharing the information. Between all of them working on the cases, maybe they'd determine the connection and solve the mystery.

Offering up information on the other two cases and the fact that I was Mr. Buckley's client gained us access to the house. As his client I would know if anything was missing. A minor fib. The place provided zero insight into the man's travels, hobbies, or family except that he collected boring artwork. Unless, of course, he spent a lot of time visiting the Black Forest in Germany. Winnie's house, on the other hand, was an open book with décor and mementos that recounted the woman's entire life.

The locked desk prevented us from snooping in drawers. No damaged wood led me to believe the intruder hadn't tried to wrench the drawers open. Hmm... We went into the bedroom. Not one item appeared out of place.

"The thief obviously didn't make it into this room."

The man's collection of black and gray designer suits hung in an orderly fashion in the closest. A large wooden case with a glass top on the dresser displayed a high-end watch collection. That was it.

"I guess the benefit of being a minimalist is if someone tosses your place, there isn't a lot of stuff to put back in order. Kind of makes me wonder if Mr. Buckley's place was frequently tossed. Or perhaps he has another place and this is merely a front. Like to throw off a thief if the lawyer has dealings with a lot of bad guys. A hideout."

Declan quirked a doubtful brow. "Think you've been watching too many movies. I wouldn't be hanging thousands of euros in artwork on my walls in a house that was a front."

My mind raced with all kinds of wild ideas. Still, the house gave me a weird vibe, like something was off—besides the fact the break-in seemed staged.

"He likely spends most of his time at work. We should pay his office a visit. Find out when they last saw him and let someone know about his house. After all, I'm a client. I have the right to know why he isn't returning my calls."

Maybe his office held clues.

Buckley, Wallace, and Hammond. I knew the law firm's name from Mrs. Muir's confirmation of receipt. However, it looked even more impressive in large gold letters displayed on the side of a glass building. A familiar black-and-white framed photograph of a tree hung behind the desk outside of Fintan Buckley's office. It looked like it was growing up from his assistant's head. Ella McDonald had dark hair pulled back in a twist, dark glasses, and a dark suit. The place obviously had a dress code. Dress like your boss, Mr. Buckley.

Ella shook her head, glancing around at the empty waiting room. "I haven't heard from Mr. Buckley in two days."

"Is that common for him to go days without at least checking in with you?"

She shrugged. "He did it once before. He didn't have any appointments that I had to cancel, which is also a bit odd. As if he knew he might be gone but didn't want to tell me." Panic filled her blue eyes. "Do you think I'll be in trouble for not having filed a missing person's report?"

"No worries." Declan flashed her a reassuring smile, which she returned with a shy one. "Who's to say he's missing?"

She nibbled on her lower lip. "I can't believe his house was broken into."

"Actually, there were no signs of a break-in, but I'd assume someone with a key wouldn't damage his belongings," I said.

She nodded faintly. "Of course not. Can't imagine someone *without* a key damaging his place. He's very well liked and a fierce nice man." She gave Declan a fleeting glance.

"He was supposed to forward my employer, Winnie Dunne, a copy of a handwritten letter from Clara O'Shea."

Ella's breath caught in her throat at the mention of the woman. "The O'Sheas are important clients."

"Could you maybe see if it's in his office?"

More lip nibbling. She nodded and went into the man's office, shutting the door behind her before we could sneak a peek.

"Wait for me downstairs," I told Declan. "I can't decide if you're making her nervous or it's something else. Like the fact that she's not telling us everything she knows."

"I could try being a bit less charming." He gave me a sly smile. "Fine. I'll be in the lobby."

Ella returned a few minutes later, shaking her head. "Sorry. Didn't see the letter. I'll mention it in my message to him. Had planned to try ringing him again later today."

"Do you have any idea where he'd go to get away?"

Vacation home on Achill Island, flat in London...

"He doesn't get away."

I believed that.

I showed her the photos of the sketches on my phone. "Do any of these people look familiar? Like maybe they were recent clients or visitors of Mr. Buckley's?"

Without hardly glancing at the photos, Ella shook her head. "No, have never seen any of them." A glint of recognition in her blue eyes and her nails tapping nervously against the desk didn't convince me.

"Could you please take another look?"

One more quick glance and she shook her head more vigorously.

She was hiding something.

Was she afraid to admit she recognized one of the people even if it meant saving her boss's life? Maybe she feared for her *own* life. Or didn't want to betray his confidence and get her boss in trouble. Mr. Buckley had no photos of family or friends at his house. If he was to confide in someone, maybe it would be a dedicated assistant. Besides your garbage man and mailman, who knew your life and schedule better than a personal assistant?

Ella definitely knew more than she was telling me.

Michael smiled brightly when we walked into Winnie's hospital room. "She touched my hand and tried opening her eyes. It was alongside her right there on the bed." He pointed to his hand resting on top of the white linens.

I placed my fingertips on the woman's wrinkled hand with an IV taped down on top. Her eclectic array of rings had been removed. "Hey, Windiana, how you doing?"

"Put her favorite lipstick on her," Michael said. "Thought it might perk her up when she does come to. Once heard that in hard times, lipstick sales soar."

The bright-pink lipstick gave Winnie's pale complexion a bit of color.

I smiled. "Looks lovely." When I was working at the estate, I couldn't live without my magenta lip gloss. Regardless of whether I was working out of the house or at home, I should be wearing the colorful gloss.

"She's the best genealogist I've ever known. Always picking up on the smallest clues. She once traced a man who changed his last name a half dozen times, including using his middle name, which was also his mother's maiden name, and a grandmother's first name. His children were all baptized in different churches because he hadn't married." He shook his head in awe of Winnie's brilliance. "Wouldn't want her looking for me if I didn't want to be found. She should be working to find violent criminals instead of heirs."

Hopefully, she'd wake up soon and help solve this case.

I motioned for Michael to follow us out into the hallway. I brought him up to speed that Patricia was Eleanor O'Shea's daughter, heir to the entire estate. And about our visit to Mr. Buckley's house and office.

"Why would someone have staged a break-in at Fintan Buckley's house?" I said.

"Because he's guilty." Michael stamped his cane on the tile floor. "He did it to make himself look innocent, then framed poor Winnie to take the fall. To get the garda off his tracks." His cheeks reddened. "Never liked the man. Not one bit."

"Why's that?" Declan asked.

"Winnie thought he could do no wrong, but I knew he could."

"Is it you don't be liking him because Winnie does?" Declan asked.

"Of course not. Don't trust him. The man is all about perception and what he wants others to believe."

"Are you sure you're being unbiased?" I asked.

He gave me a sharp nod.

"Ask around and see what other genealogists know about him," I said. "If you can find any dirt on the man."

"Be happy to."

I wouldn't be surprised if the charming Mr. Buckley turned out to be dodgy. Status and money appeared quite important to him, and I could see him betraying a client for both. Even if it was one of his oldest, and supposedly dearest, ones.

Twelve

I PICKED up my car from the hospital parking lot and followed Declan home. When we pulled into the driveway, Rachel was weeding the flower beds in front of the Coffey cottage. Mac was lying in the sun supervising. The lavender powder was out of her hair, and she was dressed in jeans and a yellow T-shirt. I hoped she hadn't spent all day pulling weeds rather than getting her wedding accounts in order. At least she'd showered, and at the side of the house white sheets hung on the clothesline, flapping in the wind.

I hopped out of the car.

Rachel stood, tilting her face toward the sun. "It was too gorgeous to stay inside." She glanced around. "It's so peaceful here. I can see why you wanted to escape the estate."

Actually, I'd wanted to escape *Rachel* more so than the estate, yet here she was. Hopefully, she wasn't thinking about permanently escaping the estate.

"There's just something so grounding about this place. It puts life in perspective." She sucked in some fresh air and slowly eased it out. "Being here has me thinking about getting my own place. I spend my time in Ireland at Gerry's townhouse in Dublin and in England at George's. I need a place just for me. Like a little English cottage where I can go home at night and separate my work life from my personal one."

"That's a great idea." Rachel had never had a personal life until the past year. She needed to continue pursuing one.

"A cottage with a yard and garden. I sat in the fairy garden and organized my emails into client folders and wrote down my voicemail messages. The accounts are ready to be handed off to Gretchen."

"Yay!" I clapped. "Did you talk to her today?"

"Checked in to see how she's doing but thought it better to go over the accounts in person."

Fingers crossed that Gretchen didn't quit because the workload was way more than what we'd discussed. She'd taken the job on a quiet English estate for a reprieve from the hectic planner life.

"So you're heading back tomorrow?"

Rachel shrugged. "Was thinking about it. Or maybe the next day. It's weird I haven't heard from Gerry."

If she was waiting an extra day to give Gerry more time to show up here, I'd give him an immediate call.

"I'm only an hour away from him. You'd think he'd have stopped by to check on me. I can't believe he hasn't even called."

"Did you tell him you're here?"

"No, but I'm sure someone did." She slid me a sideways glance. "Have you talked to him?"

I shook my head. "This is another reason you need a balanced lifestyle. To show Gerry he means more, or at least as much, to you as work. I think we should cancel the teas after September. People don't book them that far out, so there aren't many reservations yet for October."

"I think I love him," Rachel blurted out. "No, I *know* I do."

I snapped my head back in surprise. "Have you told him?"

She shook her head. "I've never said 'I love you' to any guy."

"You should tell him that also when you do say it."

"Only one guy has ever said he loved me. My response? 'I was afraid of that.' Needless to say, we broke up. What if Gerry has a similar response? I don't think I could handle the rejection right now."

"I guarantee you he won't. You have to take the chance. No relationship is easy. Look what Declan and I have been through, and now we're getting married." A goofy smile spread across my face. "A year ago who'd have thought you and I'd both end up with gorgeous Irish lads and Irish citizenship?"

"Hopefully, I still end up with him."

"You will."

"And speaking of your and Declan's wedding..."

"How about *not* speaking of it? The last thing you need is one more wedding to plan right now. It might be best if we elope."

Rachel's eyes widened. "There's no way you're eloping. Don't even joke about that."

"Maybe I'm not joking."

"You better be joking about not joking."

I held up a hand. "I'm not. The estate is booked for the fall, and I don't want to wait until spring."

I didn't? Since when?

Rachel smiled. "I have one September date on hold just in case you said that."

"What happened to crazy women expecting to plan their entire weddings only a month out? I can't plan a wedding in four weeks." Especially when all I knew was that I wanted my unidentified bridesmaids to wear magenta. To borrow something blue from Fanny. And to wear Grandma's brooch and likely a magenta hat. If I admitted these were the only ideas I had, Rachel might plan the rest of the details with or without my input.

"Fine. Where would you elope to?"

I gestured toward the cottage.

Rachel laughed. "Now you're joking."

I remained silent.

"Seriously? You'd get married *here*?"

"You were just telling me how grounded you feel here and how it changed our lives."

"Yeah, speaking of ground"—she gestured to the patches of grass and dirt—"if it rained before the wedding, we'd be standing in mud. Your dress would be ruined, and your heels would sink into the ground."

What dress? What heels?

"And if it rained during the wedding, all the guests would have to try to squeeze inside the musty cottage. George would end up with pneumonia again, and Mom's allergies would go berserk."

What guests? I hadn't even started a guest list or looked at one invitation.

"If we elope, guests aren't invited."

Rachel stared at me in disbelief. "I can't believe you'd get married without me there. So much for a gorgeous sunny day." She stalked up the drive toward the house.

"Don't you dare say a word!" I shouted after her.

I didn't want Declan to find out about my cottage wedding venue from Rachel, especially not in her foul mood.

She marched inside, and moments later her guest room door slammed shut. Phew. She hadn't mentioned our argument to Declan, who was now peering out the window at me. I shrugged, giving him a palms up. *No clue.*

My phone dinged the arrival of an email.

Clara O'Shea's cousin Peggy responded to my request for a visit. She confirmed 10:00 a.m. the following day. My email to her had been vague, merely stating that I had some news to discuss about Clara's estate. I'd apparently piqued the woman's interest. She was the daughter of Clara's first cousin, so I assumed she was under sixty-five, likely not the Mrs. Muir impostor. However, she could be the woman who'd swiped the hatbox. If she was, she wouldn't have agreed to meet with me. Unless she was setting me up.

Either way, I'd know tomorrow.

The next morning, rather than avoiding me by leaving at the crack of dawn to catch the early ferry to Wales, Rachel remained in bed. I knocked on her door and told her she'd better not be back to dousing herself in lavender dust while watching Mac and that her voicemail had better be cleaned out by the time we returned from Galway. I sounded like my mother knocking on my bedroom door during summer vacation when we were growing up. "Don't sleep in until noon again today, and that room better be cleaned by suppertime." Mom had never knocked on Rachel's door before leaving for work unless it was to remind her to make sure *I* did whatever Mom had told me to do that day.

Even when I wasn't the one behind the wheel, driving on the narrow Galway roads made me a nervous wreck. Stones replaced the hedge fences that bordered most roads and divided fields in the Midlands. If a car went over the center line—when there was one—a driver had to make a split-second decision whether to hit the car or the stone wall. An accident could shut roads down for hours, since the cars would block any through traffic. Thankfully, Declan was a skilled driver.

A paved drive cut through the sprawling 350-acre O'Shea estate, leading to a stately home three to four times the size of George's. A red Alfa Romeo convertible sat on the pavement encircling a large fountain. The place had curb appeal, except for the scraggly looking bushes. Thomas's towering statuesque shrubs at the estate would put these to shame.

We stepped from the car, and my stomach tightened. "She must know about Patricia having inherited the entire estate and her true identity, right?"

Declan shrugged. "You'd certainly think so. Would guess that was all disclosed at the reading of the will."

"I doubt they were happy to learn the estate went to some person they hadn't even known existed."

Declan gave my hand a reassuring squeeze. "You'll be grand. If this woman resembles one of the two from the sketch, we'll run our arses off."

"Maybe you should stay in the car and keep it running just in case."

"You're not going in there on your own." He rang the doorbell.

A tall, thin woman in her early sixties, dressed in an elegant pink silk shirt and tan slacks, answered the door. No visible injury from Winnie's stone necklace and not the Mrs. Muir impostor or the hatbox woman from the plane. Unless this woman was impersonating Peggy O'Shea to give us a false sense of security and lure us inside to all three sketchy people waiting for us in the living room.

I introduced myself and Declan.

The woman gave me a pleasant smile. "Ah, right, then, please come in."

We stepped into a large black-and-white tiled foyer where red-and-black modern artwork filled the white walls. Modern art wasn't my style. However, I liked it better than the black-and-white photos of trees on every one of Mr. Buckley's walls.

"Please follow me." Peggy's voice echoed up the sweeping staircase as she led us into the adjoining living room.

My shoulders relaxed upon entering the vacant room with white leather furniture bordering a red rug. A white fireplace hadn't a speck of soot on it. The room looked like an exhibit in a modern art museum. *Living Space in Red and White.* Before sitting down, I scanned the photos on the top of a black grand piano. None of the people resembled the three sketches.

We established that Peggy was aware of Patricia's identity, and I explained her medical condition. "I wasn't sure if you'd heard from Mr. Buckley or Garda Sweeney."

She shook her head, concern creasing her brow. "Very odd that Fintan wouldn't have contacted us about the woman."

I agreed. Was the man riddled with guilt?

"Not merely because our family has been his client for years, but he's a compassionate man." She continued shaking her head. "How awful. One minute Patricia Muir has inherited an estate, and the next she's gone. Simply dreadful."

"Well, she's not *gone*."

"Yes, of course not, luv. Yet critical condition and triple-bypass surgery doesn't sound promising, does it now? This has all been such a shock since the reading of Auntie Clara's will. We referred to her as auntie even though she was technically a cousin. None of us had ever heard of Patricia Muir. Amazing how a family secret managed to be kept for so many years."

"Also, I want to let you know that the hat was stolen. I'm guessing it was insured. However, I didn't receive any insurance papers to deliver with it."

"What hat, luv?"

Not the response I'd expected.

"The magenta-and-lime-green one Patricia inherited."

"Ah, yes, that one. It was quite lovely. However, lime green turns my skin yellow. You must have the right skin tone to pull off such a color. Auntie Clara had the same coloring as me. Never understood why she bought it and then never wore it."

"I thought it was Eleanor's hat?"

"No." She gazed off into space with a pensive look. "However, Auntie Eleanor could have pulled off that shade of green. Hopefully, Patricia inherited her mother's skin tone. I didn't know Eleanor well since she was estranged from her father and lived up in Donegal. However, I was with Clara when she purchased the hat at one of her charity benefits about four years ago for five hundred euros, which is a bit of quid for a hat you're never going to wear. But it was for charity, I suppose. Not to mention the style was very art deco, and Auntie Clara definitely fancied a more modern look." She sneered at the surrounding artwork.

Was Peggy lying about the hat's history because she had stolen it and wanted me to believe it had little value? Or what if someone had donated the hat, not realizing it was worth loads? Perhaps a woman had bought it at a rummage sale or thrift shop for five bucks, then donated it to the auction. Like finding a Picasso in your relative's attic after he died.

I wasn't going to be the one to tell Peggy that the hat was indeed valuable and I'd handed it over to the thief responsible for Patricia's condition.

"Do you happen to recall what auction it was?" I asked.

Peggy shrugged. "Auntie Clara was always dragging me to those dreadful benefits. Don't get me wrong—they're for good causes, except for that one my cousin held to pay for his wedding. Who does that? Him marrying that atrocious woman certainly wasn't for the family's *benefit*."

Hmm... It sounded like that guy was in desperate need of money.

"I'd much prefer to fork over a thousand euros for a dinner ticket yet not have to attend and make boring conversation with snobs and eat one more piece of fresh salmon on a crostini."

She obviously didn't consider herself in that class, or at least not as boring.

"If I recall which benefit, I'll ring you. Like I said, it was nearly four years ago, and I believe around the holidays. Auntie Clara had insisted we both wear red. And I believe it was held in Dublin."

If I told Fanny it was a charity auction, maybe she'd recall where she'd seen the hat.

"I do hope Patricia Muir recovers, for both our sakes. The thought of being responsible for this money pit gives me a migraine. I do hope the Irish Heritage Trust will be interested in it."

That ruled out Peggy's motive for murder—wishing to remain in the home and for the home to remain in the family.

"None of your other cousins have an interest in it?"

"God no. We all inherited company shares, thankfully, but now I guess we might also inherit this monstrosity. If we do, we'll hold an estate sale, I suppose, but can't imagine much here selling."

"I would have the artwork appraised," Declan said. "It might be worth a bit of quid."

The woman let out a hearty laugh. "Auntie Clara was the artist. Doubt they'd sell for much. I'll keep one in honor of her memory, of course."

"Donate them to charity benefits in her name," Declan said.

The woman smiled. "That's a brilliant idea."

"Declan's an artist."

"Do you refinish furniture?" she asked.

He shook his head. "Sorry."

"Too bad." She gestured toward a large red cabinet with black and white splashes of paint. "That's a late eighteenth-century Louis XVI secretary desk. It had a gorgeous inlaid wood design. In its original state it would have been worth nine, ten thousand euros. Now..." She rolled her eyes. "I stayed with Auntie Clara the past few years to care for her. She was truly lovely, despite her horrific taste. However, I do think painting the furniture was to spite her father, who preferred money and status over his family. Too bad the lovely furniture took the brunt of her revenge."

Even though Clara had painted the artwork and furnishings, giving the place her personal touch, it still felt cold. Colder than George's house before we'd gotten all the dampness out and the boiler fixed.

I showed Peggy the sketches on my phone.

She studied them, then shook her head. "Sorry. Don't recognize them. Should I?"

"No. I'm not sure who they are." More distant O'Shea relations Peggy had never met?

Declan and I headed down the front path toward our car.

"Why did Clara lie about the hat having been Eleanor's? Had she felt that Patricia deserved a sentimental heirloom of her mother's, not merely the drafty estate home? And why that hat? Because it was worth millions? It certainly wasn't her favorite if Peggy never saw her wear it because lime green turned her skin yellow."

"What if the person who donated the hat hadn't known its value? Maybe the person cleaning out an estate tossed it in a St. Vinnie's box rather than the box for Sotheby's. And nobody ever realized it."

I shrugged. "Is it odd that Peggy never asked why I thought the hat was valuable?"

"She likely thought you wouldn't know a real emerald from a fake. Or just thought you were off your rocker."

"That's it!"

"You're off your rocker?"

I gave Declan a playful swat. "No. That I wouldn't know a real gemstone from a fake. However, people who attend hoity-toity charity benefits for a thousand euros a plate might be able to spot a real jewel. Even if most wouldn't, a person couldn't take the chance that someone would. The jewels had to have been fake at the event when Clara bought the hat."

Declan nodded. "You're absolutely brilliant." He leaned in and gave me a quick kiss.

"I'm going to call Fanny and tell her the hat was purchased at a charity event around Christmastime four years ago. Maybe that'll help her remember where she'd seen it before. And that'll lead us to whoever donated the hat, who can confirm it'd been worth merely a few hundred euros at the time of sale." I stopped at the car before opening the door. "I'm thinking about wearing a hat for our wedding. Do you think I should?"

"Do you fancy wearing a hat for our wedding?"

I nodded. "I think I do."

"Then you should wear one."

I smiled. "I should."

A magenta-colored hat that matched Declan's tie. At least I knew what I was wearing on my head as long as Zoe or I found the perfect hat.

Now for dressing the rest of me...

Thirteen

ON THE WAY TO see Garda Sweeney, I called Fanny and got her voicemail. It was afternoon tea time, so she was likely baking scones like a madwoman. I left a message about the hat having been bought at a holiday charity event four years ago in Dublin.

We entered the garda station, and the officer was seated at his desk. I gave him a perky smile, and he frowned. He should be more pleasant since I was still willing to share info with the cranky tight-lipped man. I told him about my visit with Peggy O'Shea and Clara having purchased the hat for five hundred euros at a charity auction.

He nodded with interest. "It could be that the jewels were indeed fake when Clara O'Shea purchased the hat but were real when you handed it over to the supposed Mrs. Muir. I agree that the guests attending a charity benefit at a thousand euros a plate would possibly know real jewels from fake ones. That leaves the question, when were the fake ones swapped out with real ones?"

I was tempted to share my theory about Mr. Buckley

staging the break-in at his house and his assistant covering for him. However, I needed more evidence before making accusations, unlike Garda Sweeney.

"Your boss, Winnie Dunne, knew the jewels value," he said.

I shook my head. "No she didn't."

He wore a hesitant look, then tossed his pen onto the desk. "Based on the number of gems on the hat in your photo, it's valued at over five million euros. The three found at Winnie Dunne's house are valued at nearly a half million."

"Wait. What do you mean the ones at Winnie's house?"

"It appears your employer was tucking away a few for herself."

I shook my head in confusion. "Are you saying Winnie knew the gemstones were real and stole three off the hat? Where did you find the jewels in her house?"

"In an envelope taped under her desktop."

"No way would Winnie have hidden a half million dollars in jewels under her desk. That is one of the first places a thief, and the garda, would look. Finding her house key is a scavenger hunt, and she routinely changes the hiding spot of her laptop. She'd have hidden them in a hollowed-out piece of peat at the bottom of the pile in the woodshed. She wouldn't have been that careless. Whoever planted the jewels either wanted them to be found by the police or by the hat thief, who may have been hunting the person down looking for them."

"Maybe someone interrupted her in the middle of hollowing out a piece of peat, so she hid the jewels in the first available spot. She didn't have time to be as clever as usual."

"Then she'd have pulled a Mac," I said. "She'd have swallowed the jewels and pooped them out later."

He looked at me like I was nuts.

It made me feel a bit better that Winnie's house likely wasn't broken into by someone looking for the emerald Mac had swallowed. Still, someone trying to frame her didn't give me a warm fuzzy either.

"Now accusing Winnie of theft besides smuggling, are ya?" Declan said. "Like you accused my fiancée?"

The officer shrugged.

"You don't have the thief or the hat to prove your ridiculous theory," I said. "And did you have a search warrant for Winnie's place?"

"The jewels were uncovered while investigating a crime scene. I didn't need a warrant."

"Exactly! The person who planted the jewels knew that. He tossed the place to make it look like a break-in so you would have to investigate and uncover the jewels."

A glint of curiosity flickered in the officer's eyes before his gaze narrowed on me. "You had no idea of the hat's value you were transporting to another country?"

"No, of course not. I wouldn't have wanted the responsibility."

"There were no insurance papers or letter of authenticity?"

"Why would I have thought it was insured when the jewels were supposedly fake?"

Declan sprang to his feet. "She's not answering any further questions without a solicitor."

I surged from my chair. "You think I need a lawyer?" My gaze darted to the officer. "*Do* I need a lawyer?"

"I don't know, Ms. Shaw. You tell me. If your employer didn't steal the jewels, then who did?"

"The hatbox was in her possession for, like, a half hour between the time Mr. Buckley dropped it off and I took it home."

"So maybe Mac didn't swallow the emerald. You were getting worried about being caught, so you claimed he did and then planted the other three at your employer's house."

"That's insane!"

Declan grasped hold of my hand and led me from the room. "No worries. Winnie will clear up all of this shite when she wakes up."

"I need to prove Winnie's innocence. If being charged with smuggling doesn't put her right back in the hospital, it might put her in her grave! And what if she doesn't wake up? I need to clear her name and reputation. I don't want the memory of Windiana Jones ruined. Michael is going to blow a gasket over these ridiculous accusations. He'll be looking for dirt on Garda Sweeney rather than Mr. Buckley."

What if I did need a lawyer? How was I going to afford that? There went my savings!

"Which reminds me, I need to return his call." I phoned Michael.

"She's awake!" Michael said.

"Ugh, are you kidding me?" I wailed.

"What's wrong?" My reaction baffled the poor man.

"I'm sorry. That's great news, just not great timing. Are you in the room with her now?" I didn't want to tell him unless he walked out into the hallway.

"Yes, and she's tired, so not sure if she'll still be awake when you get here."

I told Michael we were on our way.

"Winnie waking up might be a good thing," Declan said. "Let's hope she can identify the person who broke into her house and knocked her out."

If it was indeed Mr. Buckley, what if her affection for the man clouded her judgment and kept her from telling the truth?

"For all of Winnie's exotic travels, she could certainly have made some dodgy connections around the world." Declan pushed the elevator button for Winnie's floor. "Yet from the little I know about her, she sounds feisty. And you're right— she'd have pulled a Mac before taping jewels under her desktop."

"It's not just that it'll look really bad on my résumé that my first genealogy job was for a jewel smuggler and thief, but my gut tells me she didn't do it. She wouldn't have put me in the middle of something like this knowing the type of people we could be dealing with."

Not only did I need to prove Winnie's innocence, but my own. It was like the macaron theft in Prague all over again, except much higher stakes!

When we arrived at her hospital room, Michael was sitting next to Winnie's bed. Her long white hair covered the pillow, and she had a bit of color in her cheeks. She peered over at us through heavy eyelids and smiled. Good sign that she recognized me, especially when we'd only met once. And that her eyesight was improving. She patted the bed for me to sit next to her. I hated to drop the bomb while she was in such a fragile state, but the detective could be just minutes behind us. He wouldn't be as concerned about her welfare as I was. Better for her to get the bad news from someone who believed in her innocence.

I filled her in on everything that had happened since our phone conversation following Patricia Muir being rushed to the hospital and the hat stolen. The hatbox man had impersonated Patricia's nephew. The jewel Mac swallowed had been real despite Peggy O'Shea claiming the hat had been purchased at a charity benefit for five hundred euros. Mr. Buckley's home had also been broken into, and he'd possibly gone missing. And of course, she might be arrested for jewel smuggling and theft.

Winnie's brow furrowed in concern. "My, I do hope Patricia, Fintan, and Mac are all faring well."

"Mac's grand, and Patricia is recovering," Declan said. "Not sure about your Mr. Buckley. He's still missing as far as we know."

A faint smile curled her lips. "How exciting being accused of jewel smuggling. It's all kind of James Bond–like, isn't it now? Certainly one adventure I've never had. Imagine that. We were responsible for a multimillion-euro hat and hadn't a clue." She let out a low whistle. "Is Fintan being charged as my accomplice, or rather me as his, I'd suppose, seeing as he gave me the hat?"

"Not sure. We didn't get that far," I said.

"He's guilty as sin," Michael muttered.

Winnie shook her head. "I guarantee he isn't guilty. I've never known a more stand-up man in my life." She smiled at Michael, patting his hand resting on the bed next to her.

"Except for Michael here, of course. Being by my side every day, determined to be here when I woke up."

I wasn't as confidant about Mr. Buckley's innocence. His staged break-in was odd, and he was still missing. Possibly hiding out from the thief, who'd discovered *he'd* stolen the jewels he'd planted at Winnie's. Seeing as Winnie still held him in such high regard, she obviously didn't recall him breaking into her house.

"Do you remember anything about your attacker?"

"I don't. I came home after my walk and felt someone was in the house. As I spun around to confront the person, I yanked off my necklace and swung it out in front of me, hoping to hit him. That's the last thing I remember. Figure he got in through the conservatory window that needs fixing."

"Don't worry about the damage. Declan is an artist and will be able to repair your paintings."

Winnie's gaze darkened. "What damage? Nothing was damaged when I got home. I surely would have noticed, even with my poor eyesight, which has improved greatly with a few days of rest."

"Everything will be same as you remember by the time you get home," Michael said.

"And I still have the memories, luv," she told me. "Nobody can take those away. Well, at least not yet. Still pretty sharp. Maybe we'll have to revisit a few of those spots and make new adventures."

I smiled at the idea of visiting the exotic locales.

I showed Winnie the three sketches. "Do any of these people look familiar?"

She slipped on her reader glasses and studied the photos.

"The lad looks vaguely familiar. Might have seen him once at Fintan's office a while back."

Michael slapped his hand on knee. "I knew it. Precisely when he started making his plans to steal the hat."

Winnie ignored his accusation. "Who is he?"

"The one who tried to steal the hatbox and then showed up at Mrs. Muir's house claiming to be her nephew when she doesn't have one."

"Can't imagine why he'd have been at Fintan's office." She shook her head. "That must not be where I've seen him. And perhaps he merely looks familiar. He's a handsome fella." She glanced over at Declan. "Certainly not as handsome as your lad though." She gave him a wink. "I never did get ahold of Fintan to ask his permission about sharing more information on Patricia Muir. I wonder if he got my message."

"No worries. I found your research file and read the family background. I figured it out."

Winnie patted my arm. "I knew you were going to make a brilliant assistant."

A nurse poked her head into the room. "Garda Sweeney is here to see you if you feel up to a visit."

"He's welcome to come in," Winnie said.

"Are you sure?" I muttered as he entered the room.

"Garda Sweeney, how nice of you to check in on me. I'm grand. Doctor says I'll be out of here in a few days. I heard you found three jewels under my desk. Good thing you're a brilliant detective and realize how silly that would be of me to hide them in such an obvious place. I appreciate you putting my taxes to good use by finding whoever hid them there. Sorry to say, I'm not much help, as I haven't a clue who'd have done such a thing. I didn't see who was in the house when I arrived home." Winnie yawned and acted as if she was struggling to keep her eyes open. "Please close the door on your way out, luv." She closed her eyes, pretending to drift off to sleep.

The officer stood there dumbfounded. "Ah, I'll come back later." He turned and left.

Winnie gave me a conspiratorial wink.

We were making a great team.

Fourteen

ONCE HOME, Declan took Mac for a walk and I went upstairs to the guest room to check on Rachel. I hadn't seen her since our blowout yesterday, and I needed to fill her in on everything in case the police showed up at the door. Rachel was folding dirty clothes to pack in her suitcase. Who folded dirty clothes? I tossed the pile in my bag. That way when I unpacked, I knew what was dirty and what was clean.

Rachel gave me a faint smile, pressing the wrinkles from a folded white T-shirt. "How's Declan's cousin in Galway doing?"

"I lied. We didn't go to see his cousin. You better sit down."

Rachel's eyes widened in panic. "You're freakin' me out. What's going on?" She gasped. "Omigod. Did you elope to Galway?"

"No, we didn't elope."

Her shoulders relaxed. "If you did, I wouldn't blame you. I was kind of bitchy about—"

"Yes, you were, but we'll talk about it later. Please sit." I gestured to the bed.

Rachel sat on the lavender floral comforter. After I recounted the events that'd occurred since I'd landed in Scotland three days ago, Rachel rifled through the neatly folded clothes in her suitcase and pulled out her blood pressure monitor. She handed it to me.

"Here. You need this more than I do."

"I don't want to know what it is." I tossed the device onto the bed.

"I can't believe you never told me what was going on. I get you were worried about my meltdown, but I feel horrible. It really puts my situation in perspective."

"Your health is just as serious. You need to learn to manage your stress."

"Well, you going to prison won't help my stress."

"I'm not going to prison. Neither is Winnie. This is crazy, and I'm going to figure out who's responsible."

"I better stay here."

"No, you need to return to the estate and get things back on track."

"Yeah, I suppose. Maybe it's a good thing I booked all those weddings now that you might need a lawyer."

"I won't need a lawyer. The officer has zero evidence against me. He was just seeing if I know anything. It was obvious that I'm totally clueless."

The doorbell rang.

I glanced out the window down at Fanny waving up at me. Gerry stood next to her with his hands stuffed in his front jeans pockets, a nervous look on his face. He gave me a nod hello. I gave them a wave.

Was *anyone* still working at the estate?

I turned to Rachel on the bed. "It's Fanny and Gerry."

She sprang to her feet in total panic mode. "Gerry?" She spun toward the mirror and adjusted her lopsided ponytail. She grabbed a tube of lipstick with a trembling hand and swiped it hastily over her lips. "How do I look?"

"Wonderful." I touched up her sloppy lipstick application, and we headed toward the stairs.

Rachel's breathing quickened.

I glanced over at her. "Get a grip."

She nodded, taking a deep breath.

I walked down the steps and opened the door with a perky hello, welcoming our guests.

Rachel and Gerry locked intense gazes.

"I love you," she blurted out.

Gerry stood there shell-shocked while Fanny and I exchanged uneasy glances.

"I know I should have told you that over a romantic dinner or after hot sex." Rachel glanced over at Fanny, whose cheeks flushed red. "Sorry about the sex thing." Her gaze darted back to Gerry. "And you don't have to say—"

"I love you too." Gerry slipped his arms around Rachel and gave her a passionate kiss while Fanny and I slipped down the hallway and into the peach room.

We sat on the couch, tears streaming down our cheeks. Fanny pulled her blue hanky from her purse. I blew my nose on a napkin with Tayto crumbs from the cocktail table.

Fanny gestured to the bridal magazine on the table. "Ohh, how lovely." She inhaled a shaky breath, trying to get her crying under control. "Have you found a dress?"

I shook my head, blowing my nose. "Can I borrow something blue?"

Fanny embraced me in a hug. "Of course, dear."

A few minutes later the happy couple joined us with big smiles on their faces, whereas we were still emotional basket cases.

Fanny smiled at the couple. "I'm glad I called Gerry instead of a taxi for a ride."

Declan and Mac entered the house and joined us. Declan glanced in confusion at Fanny and me crying, then over at Gerry and Rachel wearing goofy grins.

"Rachel loves Gerry," I said.

"And he loves her." Fanny blew her nose.

"Right, then." Declan gave Gerry a pat on the back. "Congratulations. Fancy a pint?"

Gerry peered over at Rachel for approval.

"I'm not going to be the type of woman who tells the man she loves when he can or can't have a beer." She smiled.

He gave her a kiss before he and Declan headed toward the kitchen, with Mac trotting behind, one of the guys.

"You came all the way here to fix things between Gerry and me?" Rachel asked.

"Actually, that was merely one of three reasons for my visit. I need to make sure we're okay and I'm not the reason you left. I feel horrible for the way I spoke to you."

Rachel went over and sat next to Fanny. "You had the right to tell me how you felt, especially since it's your house. It was the slap in the face I needed." She gave the woman a hug. "Everyone had the right to be upset. I'd gone over the edge."

Fanny smiled. "I want the estate to be self-sufficient, but

you should both know that I have a backup plan. There's no need to be working ourselves to death for fear of losing the estate."

"Ah, about that..." Rachel confessed the number of weddings booked through the end of the year.

Fanny brushed off the news with a wave of her hand. "We'll manage. Gretchen and Nigel are perfect additions to our team. And that's what we are, a team."

"Hopefully, Gretchen feels that way after I hand over some of my wedding clients."

Fanny patted Rachel's knee. "No worries. We'll give her a nice little bonus."

Rachel nodded with a smile, rather than arguing about not having funds for employee perks.

Fanny took a deep breath. "Anyway, my big news. I drove my Aston Martin into town this past week during a vintage car show in the area. A car collector asked if I'd be interested in selling it. I told him no, that it'd been in my family for seventy years and had been my father's favorite. The man offered four million pounds for the vehicle and gave me his card should I change my mind and decide to sell."

My jaw dropped. "Four million pounds?"

"Four *million*?" Rachel muttered.

"I hadn't a clue it was worth that. If I had, Bernie knew I'd insist on doing the practical thing and sell it to invest in our retirement. He knew I adored my father and that car. Now, I'm afraid to drive it knowing what it's worth, and it would be silly to let it just sit in a garage. A car like that is meant to be driven fast and often, was what my father always said. He'd want it to be driven, even if not by me. You can't be telling George. He's too proud and would never agree to me selling it for the estate's sake. But I wanted you girls to know we have a backup plan. Besides, it would be better for my health riding around on a bicycle than in an expensive car."

"Like Cousin Enid?" Rachel smirked.

I pictured Enid pedaling furiously up the drive on a bicycle, dressed in fitted tan slacks, a black blazer, knee-high black boots, and a black helmet. She always looked like she should be riding a horse in a polo match rather than pedaling a bike. Or like the Wicked Witch of the West going after Toto.

"My Lord, I hope to never be a thing like that woman. Although I must say, she came to tea with a friend the other day and was much more pleasant than usual."

If there was hope for Cousin Enid, there was hope for anyone.

"We might need to put your backup plan into action for Caity's lawyer." Rachel glanced at me.

I shook my head at Fanny. "Don't worry—we won't."

I told her about the hat drama.

"Oh my, I'm glad your boss is recovering. I certainly hope Mrs. Muir will soon be on the mend. After receiving your message, the more I thought about it, I'm sure it was my friend Catherine who showed me that hat in an auction brochure. She's mad about hats and is always attending charity events. I must ring her and see."

Luckily, Catherine answered Fanny's call and remembered the hat. She became so heated about it that Fanny had to hold the phone out from her ear, enabling Rachel and I to listen in on the conversation. Catherine was still upset the hat hadn't gone to auction, allowing her to bid on it. That the woman who donated it, Millie Moran, could have made more by not selling it to Clara O'Shea beforehand for a mere five hundred euros. Catherine had been willing to pay at least seven hundred. She was off to locate the auction brochure and promised to send us a photo.

Fanny lowered the phone from her ear and rolled her eyes. "That's why the hat stuck in my head. Catherine went on about it for months after the auction. I'm surprised she didn't ask about my interest in it just now, wondering if it might be going up for auction again. I won't be telling her it was stolen. She'll insist such a thing never would have happened if she'd bought the hat. And then I'll have to listen to that for months."

Excitement raced through me. "This is a huge clue, Fanny. Having the auction photo to compare to mine will confirm the jewels weren't the same ones as when Clara O'Shea bought the hat."

Within five minutes, Catherine texted Fanny several hat photos, including close-up shots from the auction booklet. Starting bid was two hundred euros. I compared the photos to the one on my phone.

Fanny squinted through her reader glasses at the photos. "They look the same to me."

Rachel and I nodded in agreement.

"Identical." I dropped back onto the couch. "That means someone didn't swap out the jewels after Clara bought it for a mere five hundred euros."

Fanny tapped a finger against her pink lips. "Interesting that none of the bidders had the opportunity to view the hat in person because Clara purchased it prior to the benefit. I assure you, Millie Moran knew the value of that hat. The woman just paid an extraordinary amount for an emerald necklace at a Sotheby's auction. She knows her jewels."

Where had I heard the name Millie Moran lately?

"Why wouldn't that Millie woman have wanted to get every cent she could for charity?" Rachel asked.

Fanny grasped my forearm. "Blackmail. Clara O'Shea must have been blackmailing Millie Moran for millions. What dirt did she have on the woman?"

"This is sounding like a *Sunnyvale* episode," Rachel said.

Fanny's brow furrowed. "But if it was worth that much, Clara would certainly have wanted provenance detailing the history of the hat's ownership. In this case it would have been the auction brochure and payment receipt for a mere five hundred euros. After the fact, any jeweler could have done a proper appraisal and adjusted the value. Why else would both women know the hat's value but agree on such a low price?"

"Someone could have seen the hat either on Clara or in the brochure and knew its value, and stolen it," Rachel said.

I shook my head. "I doubt you can tell the jewels are real just from the photo. And Peggy said Clara never wore the hat, that she's aware of."

Fanny wore a pensive look. "It still makes no sense that someone framed Winnie with three gemstones. Whoever broke into her house was either planting the jewels or looking for them. If searching for them, it must have been an inept thief not to have found them. What then? He went to Mr. Buckley's thinking maybe he'd stolen them?"

"Mr. Buckley is somehow mixed up in all of this," I said.

"You must pay Millie Moran a visit and ask the daft woman why she sold a five-million-euro hat for five hundred euros," Fanny said. "And see her reaction when you inform her it was stolen. To think my beloved Aston Martin is worth about the same as that hat."

"Millie Moran..." I tried to place the name. Mildred, not Millie! "Is Millie's name actually Mildred?"

Fanny shrugged. "Suppose it probably is."

"Is her family in the hotel industry?"

"Walter Moran was one of the wealthiest hoteliers in the UK. Passed away maybe twenty years ago, but the company is still in business."

"What if the hat was indeed a family heirloom, merely not the family everyone thought? Everyone except for Winnie, that is. She was closing in on the truth behind Patricia's biological father. The hat could be from *his* family, not Eleanor O'Shea's." I snatched Winnie's computer off the desk. "She has a Notes document with scanned newspaper clippings about Walter Moran and Thomas O'Shea's falling-out as business partners and some articles from the social column."

I opened the document, Fanny and Rachel leaned in, and we scanned the clippings. "I recall something about Walter's children being Mildred and Edward, who both attended St. Andrews. In the O'Shea biography it mentioned Eleanor graduated from there. Patricia's biological father was noted as John Kelly on the birth record. One of the most common Irish names. Had to have been thousands with that name at the time, except for Patricia's dad. Maybe Eleanor chose that name for anonymity purposes and the father was really Edward. The child, Patricia Mildred, was named after her aunt and possibly Eleanor's best friend. It's interesting that the adoptive parents kept the birth name."

"The children apparently weren't archenemies despite

the fathers' professional rivalry," Rachel said. "Yet why would Clara buy a five-million-euro hat from Millie for five hundred euros?"

My fingers flew across the keyboard. "I bet the university has an alumni list online or on a genealogy site." Within minutes I was scrolling through graduates starting with the year Patricia was born. "In the spring quarter 1958, Edward Moran graduated with a degree in history. No Eleanor O'Shea. That's the year Patricia was born, so Eleanor's degree had likely been delayed. Sure enough, Eleanor graduated in the fall quarter 1958 with a degree in elementary education."

"Forbidden love," Rachel said. "Like Grandma and Michael Daly. How sad."

"According to one headline, Edward Moran became partner at his father's business five years later. While Eleanor had moved back to Ireland and become a teacher. Never married or had more children." The article had a picture of the dashing young Edward.

Fanny wiped a tear from her cheek. "How tragic."

I nodded, swallowing a lump of emotion in my throat.

Rachel cupped a hand over her mouth, stifling a sob.

"My gut tells me Edward was Patricia's father and Winnie believes the same thing," I said.

"Why would Clara and Millie have been so secretive about the hat?" Rachel asked.

"The two women wanted to right a wrong." Fanny clapped her hands together. "As simple as that. Perhaps they felt Edward and Eleanor had been treated badly by both families making them give their child up for adoption. They assumed other relations would contest the inheritance if they knew the hat's value, so the two conspired to pretend the hat had no value."

I nodded, trying to piece it together in my head. "Millie is quite possibly the only person left alive who knows the truth. I need to pay her a visit. Clara bought the hat four years ago. Had it always been their plan to find Patricia and give her the hat, or had there initially been another reason for it? Winnie was hired to locate Patricia. She was known for solving dinosaur cases. Maybe this was one of them. Clara had maybe hired other genealogists who'd failed."

"The Moran estate is in Yorkshire, about two hours east of our estate," Fanny said. "We can all journey back to England tomorrow, and you and Declan can pay her a visit."

Should I reach out to Millie Moran first, or would the element of surprise be in my favor?

Fifteen

THE NEXT MORNING Declan dropped Mac off at his parents' before he, Fanny, Rachel, and I took the ferry to Wales. We followed each other for two hours, until Fanny and Rachel headed north to the Daly estate in Lancashire and we headed east through Yorkshire to visit Millie Moran.

During the drive, I called Michael and confirmed our patient was doing well. The doctor planned to release Winnie in two days. I needed to get this solved so we could clean up and repair the damage at Winnie's before her arrival home. Michael planned to start on it today. Hopefully, Millie Moran would provide us with the needed clue to solve the entire mystery.

Fanny was right—Millie loved her jewels. The Irish woman sat across from Declan and me in a brown leather wingback chair, dressed in a deep-blue pantsuit that matched her sparkly sapphire earrings. According to Declan, the original Renoir in a gilded frame hanging over the fire-place was worth five times the earrings. I was glad we'd spiffed up for the visit. Declan was dressed in black slacks, a white button-down shirt, black vest, and pink-and-gray tie. He'd look great in a magenta tie at our wedding. I wore a white chiffon dress with pink polka dots. Still, I felt under-dressed compared to Millie. I should have at least worn my gold hoop earrings.

"Thank you so much for seeing us on such short notice," I said. "I have to admit, I wasn't completely up front on the phone about wanting to discuss you making a donation for an upcoming charity benefit. I'm interested in a hat you donated to one four years ago."

Except for a slight twitch in Millie's cheek, her expression remained unreadable.

"Clara O'Shea hired my employer, Winnie Dunne, to locate the biological daughter of her sister, Eleanor, which she did."

Millie's brow raised slightly.

"I was responsible for delivering part of an inheritance to Clara's niece, Patricia Muir, in Scotland."

Millie's gaze narrowed slightly.

Had I discovered the hat's authentic jewels, the identity of Patricia's father, or both?

I recounted the story up to Patricia's heart attack and then the hat and letter vanishing.

The woman's hand snapped to her chest. "How dread-ful. I thought it curious that I hadn't heard from the woman after she read Clara's letter. And with Clara now gone, nobody knew to contact me. I'll make sure that Patricia is receiving the best care possible."

"Her daughter returned from Australia to be with her."

"Ah, grand." Millie raised a curious brow. "I'm assuming during your employer's search for Eleanor's biological daughter that she uncovered the identity of Patricia's father? That you're not merely here about the hat?"

"Your brother Edward?" I asked.

She nodded. "Who would your employer have told about Patricia's identity or the hat?" Millie demanded.

"Nobody, I guarantee." I explained Winnie's condition and how she'd also ended up in the hospital. "The only other person outside of the O'Sheas who knows is Mr. Buckley, who's been the family's solicitor for decades. And any of your relations who were told."

"Nobody was told. Why in the world would someone do such a thing?"

"The hat. When I learned that Clara O'Shea had purchased your expensive hat for merely five hundred euros at a charity auction, I found it interesting considering your families' pasts, which I recently discovered from newspaper clippings. It just seemed like there had to be more of a connection there and why the hat changed family hands for so little."

"What makes you believe the hat was worth more than five hundred euros?"

I was afraid my story about Mac pooping out one of the hat's lovely emeralds would give this elegant woman a stroke, yet I went with the truth. Rather than gasping in horror, she let out an amused laugh.

"Clara would have found that story humorous. She was a carefree spirit and loved a good prank. Much more of a rule breaker than Eleanor or I ever were." She pressed back in her chair with a sigh. "It's actually a relief to not be keeping that secret after seventy-two years. That I'm no longer the only living person who knows not only the identities of Patricia's parents but their tragic story. Clara had included that all in the letter. How sad that it's gone missing."

I was more determined than ever to find that letter!

"Eleanor and I were great friends growing up. We were a few years older than Clara, so she had younger playmates during the summers at our families' resort in Kerry." She stared into the fireplace, a look of longing and a faint smile on her face. "Edward considered me his bratty little sister, even though we were only a year apart. He taught Nellie—Eleanor—and me to play golf at the resort. He was obsessed with the sport and dreamed of becoming an instructor. Of course, our father would never have allowed him to *waste* his life on golf. So Edward planned to attend St. Andrews to study history and business to appease father and work at the renowned golf course without his knowledge. The summer before he started at university, Eleanor confided in me her love for Edward. That was no surprise. She lit up every time she saw him and was nearly a better golfer than him, always out on the course pretending it was the game she loved, not my brother. Then the wall went up. And our lives changed forever." She shivered despite sitting directly in the sunshine streaming in through the open drapes.

"The wall?" Declan asked.

"The revenge wall. After a heated argument, Thomas O'Shea bought out my father's shares in the property. My father used the money to purchase the land next door and to build a taller hotel strategically positioned that cast an afternoon shadow over the other hotel's swimming pool. Everyone knows how important it is to bask in what little sunshine Ireland does have. My father was a nasty man, putting his former best friend Thomas O'Shea out of business."

"How horrible," I muttered.

"Despite our fathers forbidding us children to be friends, Nellie and I pursued our plans to attend St. Andrews. Our mothers knew and remained quiet to spite their husbands, who'd broken up their friendship. They'd honored their husbands' wishes that they no longer communicate, which was devastating for them both."

I couldn't imagine my parents forbidding me to marry Declan. Suddenly I wanted to marry him ASAP!

"Edward attended the university also, and the two of them fell madly in love. They'd sit for hours in a café, talking about history, boring me to tears. They were passionate about education and each other."

"Patricia is a retired teacher," I said

Millie smiled. "Eleanor would be over the moon. And about the family history being passed on to her daughter. I pray the hat will be also."

"We'll find the hat," I assured her.

"My mother referred to it as her 'rainy-day' hat. As you can see, my father had a surly disposition. My mother made sure she had a safety net should he ever leave her. It gave her a sense of satisfaction and control knowing she could stand on her own if needed. She was walking around with five million euros on her head without him having a clue. However, she never wore the hat except in the house, for fear a jeweler or gemstone expert would realize the stones were genuine. Father was too absorbed in work to notice a pair of emerald or sapphire earrings missing here and there. Over the years, she pieced that hat together. One day she caught me playing dress-up in her bedroom, wearing the hat. I'd never seen my mother so angry. I burst into tears. She felt horrible about the incident still years later and explained the importance of her rainy-day hat. My mother swore me to secrecy. She believed women in those days had to watch out for themselves. She hoped we'd have more rights and equality in the future and that divorce would be a more acceptable option for women. The hat was to be passed down to an heir who might one day need to cash in the jewels. She made me promise to do so."

"If you don't mind me asking, why hadn't you looked for Patricia sooner?"

"Eleanor was against searching for her daughter. She felt she'd failed her child by not standing up to her father. Then shortly after putting Patricia up for adoption, she left home, never to speak to him again. I shared the secret about the hat with Clara years ago, and we attempted to find Eleanor's daughter but failed to locate her. With more available records and advancements in genealogy research, we recently revisited our quest. Ten years ago Clara and I took DNA tests, without success to this day. Patricia and her descendants must not have tested."

"Why did you decide to pass the hat to Clara and take the chance of the jewels being discovered?"

"A few years ago, I fell quite ill but miraculously recovered. I placed it in the charity auction to establish a low value and transfer it to Clara without raising suspicions with other relations. Patricia would surely have had to sell the hat to pay taxes, and that defeated the hat's purpose."

"Speaking of relations." I showed Millie the photos of the sketches. "These three were involved with the hat's theft. Do you recognize any of them?"

She shook her head. "Sadly, I don't."

How couldn't one of these three people be a relation of Millie Moran's or Peggy O'Shea's? Unless a relation had hired them to do the dirty work. What if Mr. Buckley read the letter and discovered the paternal connection, then made a deal with dodgy relations to split the earnings? If that wasn't the case, what was?

I needed to further question the lawyer's assistant, Ella. I was certain she knew at least one of the people in the sketches.

By the time Declan and I reached the Daly estate, afternoon tea had ended. Place settings had been cleared from the library, and everyone was taking a break before resetting the room for the next morning's tea. Perfect timing. Cocktail time.

Fanny was relaxed on her blue fainting couch with her shoes off, chatting with George and Rachel. Nigel and Declan sat on the blue velvet couch across from Gretchen and me. The former hotel banquet captain had exchanged his black suit, crisply pressed tie, and white dress shirt for tan slacks and a cream-colored button-down. His brown tweed blazer was draped over the couch's arm.

"I like your more relaxed look," I told Nigel.

"No suit *suits* me quite well, I'd say. And should you once again require assistance in proving your innocence, I am up to the task." He swiped his hands through the air, performing karate moves. His refined English demeanor had relaxed as well.

"You know *I* can also take down a thief." Gretchen laughed. "Even in a dress." Her casual green floral sundress with a cropped white cardigan was very Laura Ashley. Unlike the old Gretchen.

"Who'd have thought I'd go from stealing macarons to jewels? Does that mean I'm moving *up* in the world, or *down*?"

"Definitely up, I like to think." Declan struck a debonair pose in his vest and his loosened pink tie, giving me a sly grin.

I flashed him a flirty smile.

"This is quite different than the hotel boardroom table Nigel, Gretchen, and I sat around six months ago." I gestured to the scarred antique wooden cocktail table displaying our crystal wineglasses filled with a smooth cabernet. "I sat through a grueling two-hour food and beverage meeting without a clue, jotting down Gretchen's demands. She gave the exact number of coffee and tea gallons for each meal function. Made changes to every room setup diagram. Reiterated a dozen times that the refrigerated product cage must remain locked at all times and only Nigel and she were to have keys. And anyone found accessing the product without permission would be guillotined in Prague's Old Town Square when the astronomical clock struck midnight."

Gretchen gave me a playful swat. "I did not say that." Her smile faded. "Did I?"

"No, dear, but we got the message loud and clear." Nigel sliced a hand across his throat.

"Yet Nigel remained unflappable," I said. "While my palms were sweating so bad, I could barely hold on to my pen."

"Still, if I remember correctly, you referred to Gretchen

as a food and beverage goddess."

Gretchen's green eyes widened in surprise. "Seriously?"

I shrugged. "Well, you were."

"Still are," Declan said. "Never worked with anyone who knows catering like you."

"Thank you." She gave Declan a pleased look rather than a seductive one, like she used to. The one that always had me acting like an insanely jealous girlfriend even before we were dating.

"In all fairness to me, Blair's event orders were always a nightmare," Gretchen said. "She expected me to nail everything down once on site because she hadn't a clue how to plan food and beverage events." Gretchen snatched her wine off the table and took a calming gulp. "I'm so lucky I didn't end up having a stroke on half the meetings I worked. Here's to no more batshit-crazy planners in our futures." She took another drink of wine.

I glanced over at Rachel chatting with Fanny and George, relaxed in a comfy red chair, sipping her wine.

"We've all had our meltdowns," Gretchen said. "Hers doesn't begin to compare to what I've dealt with over the years. And she's back on track. Besides my friend's stroke, what really got me on track was you." Gretchen smiled at me. "Learning my paternal family history gave me a sense of my past, which helped give my future a direction."

Nigel nodded. "Indeed. I'm thinking that telling my aunt her father was sent off to a penal colony might be what she needs to bring her down a few notches and make my life easier."

We all laughed.

"Thanks to genealogy, I found my uncle George," I said.

"That you did." George joined our conversation from where he was seated. "And changed my life for the better. Thanks to you, I am still living on the estate. Found my Coffey relations and the love of my life." He smiled at Fanny. "And I'm on amicable terms with Cousin Enid, which is possibly the biggest miracle of all."

"The estate is a meeting planner rehab slash genealogy retreat," I said. "Genealogy could help give planners a new perspective on life and what really matters."

"Actually, the Coffey cottage was my rehab facility," Rachel said. "Funny how your dead ancestors breathe new life into you."

I raised my wineglass. "Here's to our ancestors."

Everyone raised their glasses in toasting.

"I wasn't ever a planner, but the estate turned me into one, or I might have lost it," George said. "I enjoy the events, but a bit more in moderation would be nice."

"Here's to moderation." Fanny held up her wineglass, and we toasted to downsizing our crazy schedule.

Declan and I had to be up early to catch the first ferry. Upon arrival in Dublin, we were heading straight to Fintan Buckley's office. We'd interrogate his assistant, Ella, until she confessed what she knew about her boss's dodgy dealings. So we said our good nights and goodbyes and went to bed before the others. After killing several bottles of wine, everyone decided now that the estate was fully staffed, they'd have time to reset for tea in the morning.

Declan lay with feather pillows propping him against the

headboard of the four-poster bed with a blue quilt. He was catching up on his client correspondence while I emptied the silver bucket filled with rainwater into the porcelain pedestal sink in our bathroom. I replaced the bucket on the hardwood floor beneath the ceiling's brown water stain. I'd often lain in bed at night listening to rain drip into the bucket, anticipating water gushing from the ceiling. By the end of the year, the roof would be replaced, the ceilings repaired.

I removed a blue knitted blanket from the back of the rocking chair in the corner and shook it out. I pictured Grandma rocking George to sleep in the wooden chair when he was a baby. She'd left for America when he was only two. Sadly, she might never have had the chance to watch her son playing on the wooden rocking horse next to the chair.

I hopped into bed with the blue afghan. "It's so sad that Eleanor's and Edward's families kept the two of them apart. I'm glad that my grandma and Michael Daly chose to be apart from their families rather than each other. However, in the end both couples gave their only child up for adoption."

"We'll certainly never give our child up for adoption."

I glanced over at Declan. "We're having a child?"

"More than one, I hope." His gaze darted to me. "Why? Don't you be wanting wee ones?"

"Before genealogy and you, I was never sure. Now I can't imagine not having children to pass on our legacy. It would make me so sad if Patricia didn't have a daughter to inherit her hat. If we find it."

"We'll find it."

"I don't want to elope or get married at the Coffey cottage."

He quirked a brow. "The Coffey cottage?"

"Was just a thought. I want to get married here. George and Fanny started a family tradition I want to continue and want our children to continue. We'll hold the ceremony outside so I don't have to worry about falling down the staircase. And I'd prefer not to be married in the same room as the TV couple. One benefit of Rachel having conducted so many site inspections is she knows all the bridal vendors and can likely find an available photographer, caterer, and decorator on short notice."

"How short of notice?"

"A month."

"Sounds brill. Mac, of course, will be the ring bearer."

"How do you feel about a magenta-colored tie?"

"Sounds grand. Gerry could pull off the color."

"Rachel would look great in it also. How many fellas were you thinking to have stand up?"

"Just Gerry. What were you thinking?"

"That sounds perfect. I'd like to keep it small. And if I have Fanny, I'd want to have Zoe, and I don't want the wedding party to end up bigger than the guest list." I was too tired to even begin discussing the invites. I leaned over and gave Declan a warm kiss.

"Maybe we should start working on those children." He rolled onto his side toward me with a steamy look that set my body on fire. He gently touched his lips to mine, giving me a teasing kiss.

I drew my head back slightly, gazing deep into his dreamy blue eyes, breathing heavily. "How about we just practice for now?"

"Practice is good, even though I think we've perfected it."

I agreed. We were perfect together in every way.

Sixteen

THE NEXT DAY Declan and I went straight from the Dublin port to Mr. Buckley's office in a northern suburb. According to the main receptionist, Ella, was due back from lunch shortly. We took a seat in the waiting area across from Ella's desk. I stared at the black-and-white photo of a lone tree hanging on the wall.

I shook my head. "I don't understand his obsession with photos of trees."

Declan tilted his head to the side, studying the framed artwork. "Well, many do, since the photographer makes loads."

"He could retire from the amount of money Fintan Buckley has dropped on his photos."

"You're awfully anti-trees for being a genealogist. Isn't ancestry research all about trees?"

"*Family* trees, which are rarely black and white. They're more like endless shades of gray."

I studied the tree from a genealogist's perspective. The short trunk had stoically supported the thick, gnarly branches for generations. This tree had character. Whereas the ones at the lawyer's home all looked similar, as if from the same forest.

Mr. Buckley exited his office, startling us, since we weren't aware he was in there. He came to an abrupt halt, and a fleeting look of panic flashed across his face before he regained his unflappable demeanor.

"Ms. Shaw, how lovely to see you. Sorry I haven't rang you back. I had to leave town on urgent business for a few days and am just now catching up." He smoothed a hand down his crisply pressed navy tie. "May I assist you with something?"

I sprang to my feet. "Assist me with something?" My high-pitched incredulous tone startled a woman walking past.

"Please step into my office."

He placed a hand firmly on my back and marched me across the lobby. I'd have been screaming for help if Declan wasn't hot on our heels. Buckley's office blinds were shut, and a dim lamp barely lit the lawyer's massive desk. At the sound of the door locking behind us, I spun around to face the man, whose eyes filled with fear.

"How's dear Winnie?" He marched over and snatched a crystal decanter from the credenza and poured himself a whiskey. "The hospital said she has regained consciousness." He loosened his tie enough to unbutton his starched white collar and then slammed his drink.

I was thrown by his frazzled behavior. If he was acting, he was Oscar material and had missed his calling.

"She's, uh, doing well. Why didn't you return my messages?"

"I hadn't a clue what was going on." He poured another drink. "I came home to find my house an utter disaster and assumed it was a disgruntled client I'd filed an order against. Shortly after, I received your message about poor Winnie and didn't know what to think. The two break-ins had to be related. I debated involving the garda but feared that falsely accusing my client would upset him even further. And if it wasn't him, I decided it best to go on radio silence in case our phones or computers were being monitored. None of this makes sense. Why would someone steal the hat and paperwork?"

I told him about the hat's jewels being real and someone planting three of them in Winnie's house.

"The jewels are authentic?" He wiped sweat from his brow and gave his collar a solid tug. "The hat must be worth millions. I had no idea. Why wouldn't Clara have told me this? Was she trying to avoid inheritance taxes on Mrs. Muir's end? She should have confided in me. I've been the O'Shea family's solicitor for forty years."

I told him Millie Moran's rainy-day hat story and that Patricia's biological father was Edward Moran.

"She hadn't told me that either. Are you sure about all this? I can't imagine her not confiding in me."

The man was losing sight of the bigger issue here. If anyone should be able to see the forest through the trees, it was Mr. Buckley.

"Yes, I'm sure, and Winnie's research is what put me onto the trail of Patricia's biological father. Peggy O'Shea didn't know the jewels were real either, if it makes you feel better."

"It's one thing not to confide in family, but I was more like family than any of those distant relations."

Speaking of rellies, I shared the photos of the sketches with him. Based on the lawyer's reaction to the entire drama, I had little hope they were his accomplices. "Do you recognize any of these people?"

"Yes, of course. That lad is my assistant's, Ella McDonald's, boyfriend."

Declan and I exchanged shocked glances. The maple nutmeg cookie guy?

"Sure about that, are ya?" Declan said.

"Yes. I've seen him dozens of times. He's usually around at least once a week to collect her for lunch."

"When was the last time you saw him?" I asked.

"Last week, I think." He shook his head in confusion, "What is this about?"

I filled him in on Ella's boyfriend impersonating Patricia Muir's nephew and trying to steal the hatbox on the plane.

"How on earth would Ella know the hat's jewels were real if I didn't? Clara certainly wouldn't have confided in her and not me."

Get over it!

"Did she have access to the hat?"

"Of course. She photographs and documents all heirlooms and items received in the office. If I'd known it was worth millions, I'd have done it myself and secured it in my safe. Not that I don't trust her. Or *did* anyway. There must be a logical explanation for this."

A knock sounded at the door. We all froze. Mr. Buckley cautiously walked over and opened the door to find Ella. He demanded she come into his office. She saw Declan and me, and her pleasant smile faded.

"Did you steal Mrs. Muir's hat?" the lawyer blurted out, as if the woman were sitting on the witness stand.

Her body went rigid, yet she attempted to recover with a baffled look, not nearly as good an actor as her boss. "Hat? Was that the purple and green—"

"Don't even try to deny it," I said. "We've got your DNA on Winnie Dunne's stone necklace." Or someone's DNA anyway.

Rather than making a run for it, Ella burst into tears and flopped onto a chair. She sobbed uncontrollably while I handed her tissues from a box.

Declan poured a whiskey for the crying woman and the stressed-out lawyer.

"I didn't mean to hurt that poor woman," she said. "How is she?"

"Recovering, no thanks to you," I snapped. "Can't believe you left her there lying on the floor."

Ella bit down on her lower lip, her eyes watering. "I was in Ms. Dunne's house returning three of the four jewels. When she heard me coming out from hiding behind the sofa, she tore off her necklace, and the beads went flying. As she turned toward me, she slipped on them. Her arm swung up when I was going to catch her, and the stone hit me in the head." She pulled back the side of her hair to reveal a gash behind her ear.

"What the bloody hell were you doing in her house?" Mr. Buckley tossed his arms in the air. "Why in the world did you have the jewels? I don't understand any of this. It's absurd."

"Start at the beginning," I said.

She gulped down half her whiskey. "My boyfriend Alfie's father owns a chain of jewelry stores in Ireland and the UK. Alfie worked there while attending university. He collected me from work the other day, and I showed him the lovely hat. I asked him what he thought of it. That I was thinking of having one made just like it for ladies' day at the races. After a closer look and holding it up to the light, he claimed the jewels were real. I didn't believe him until he assured me just one of the jewels would pay for my mum's care. She's really sick." She caught a sob in a tissue. "I knew he wouldn't lie about a way to help my mum. He said nobody would ever notice just one stone missing. I told him I'd think on it. He planned to bring one of his father's magnifiers for a better look the next day. I didn't realize Mr. Buckley was taking it to Ms. Dunne's that evening."

The man shook his head in disbelief. "And to think I trusted you implicitly."

She bit down on her lower lip again, fighting back tears. "I'm sorry." She took a sip of whiskey. "When I rang Alfie that the hat was gone, he said he'd handle it. I knew Mrs. Muir lived in a village north of Edinburgh. Alfie and his sister waited at the airport gate for an elderly woman carrying the hatbox." She glanced over at me. "Except you showed up with it instead. He recognized the hatbox. He and his sister planned to nick it when leaving the plane, then go to the nearest loo and remove a stone. Just one. And then return to the gate where they assumed you'd be telling an airline agent the cases were swapped. But you caught up with them before they had the chance to find a loo."

If I'd slipped and fallen when chasing after them, nobody would have been any the wiser about the jewels.

"Alfie had a backup plan just in case. My mum's sister lives in Glasgow. She was going to intercept the hat before you got to Mrs. Muir's. Steal the box, take a jewel, and then return it to the woman's house. That plan wasn't nearly as brilliant and didn't go as we'd hoped."

Mr. Buckley's gaze narrowed on her. "You think?"

She sank down in the chair. "My auntie was waiting across the street from Mrs. Muir's. The woman was outside gardening, when suddenly she placed a hand on her chest and appeared to be having trouble breathing. She went inside, and my auntie rushed across the street and looked in the window to see Mrs. Muir lying on the floor. The door was unlocked, so she went inside. She was calling 999 for an ambulance when she saw you walking up the street with the hatbox. She panicked and hung up as the person answered on the other end. Knowing someone would be coming to check on the woman, my auntie had to get out of there as fast as she could. She didn't have time to take off a jewel, so she took the entire hat.

"When Alfie and his sister arrived, she'd already left with the hat, and she didn't have a cell phone to ring her. He saw the police vehicle in front of the house and was going to check on what happened, when he ran into you. He didn't think you'd gotten a good look at him at the airport but figured you'd given a description of him to the police at her house."

"His cologne gave him away," I said.

Ella grimaced at something as minor as a fleeting scent

having incriminated him. "I gave him that for Christmas. It's quite lovely, isn't it?"

I nodded. Delicious. If I bought a bottle for Declan, I'd gain ten pounds from eating cookies.

"We had to divert the police's attention from Alfie to something else. We weren't thinking clearly. I figured if I returned three of the jewels to Winnie Dunne's house and the hat to Mrs. Muir's, the police might back off."

"Wait," Declan said. "Why'd you end up taking *four* jewels instead of *one*?"

"That was my auntie's fault, not ours. Not to be throwing her under the bus or anything."

She was already under that bus and been run over several times.

"I was returning the three extra jewels my auntie had taken to Ms. Dunne's and planned to anonymously tell her to check under the desk for them. When she came home and fell, Alfie said we should make it look like a break-in so it looked random."

"Why toss my home?" her boss demanded.

"I was very careful not to damage any of your framed artwork. I didn't want to get fired."

"Get fired?" Mr. Buckley let out a bitter laugh. "That should be the least of your worries. It will take me some time to get the scuffs out of the frames, and three scratched pieces of glass will have to be replaced."

"Where is the hat and the one jewel you kept?" I asked.

"In my closet at home."

Mr. Buckley's eyes widened. "You have a five-million-euro hat sitting unsecured in your apartment's closet?"

"We were going to leave it at Mrs. Muir's house, but she

was in the hospital. We didn't want to take the chance of it getting nicked."

The lawyer rolled his eyes. "Oh, the irony. Thieves worrying about a hat being stolen."

This story was crazier than my *Kitty the Kat Thief*!

And it had a better plot twist. Ella hadn't even been on my radar as the possible thief. I'd best stick to solving genealogy mysteries.

Seventeen

⁓

Two days later Winnie was home from the hospital, so I popped in for a visit. She was sitting in her purple velvet chair next to a bright lamp, squinting at a tiny teal-colored bead while slipping it onto the necklace string. Her eyesight seemed to be improving.

Hopefully, that didn't mean I was out of a job.

She took the stone from her lap and shook it in her hand. "This poor yoke has been through a lot. Good thing it's made of sturdy stock."

"Where'd you get it?" I sat on the teal couch across from her, anxious to hear if it was from an archaeological dig in Egypt or possibly her birthplace, Istanbul.

"My garden. Used it as a paperweight for years, then while looking at it one day thought it'd make a unique necklace. So I made it into one. After all, my garden is my favorite spot in the world." She gave me a wink.

"Are those from your garden?" A vase of yellow flowers sat on her desk.

She smiled at the bouquet with a blissful look on her

face. "No, those are from Micky. Such a lovely man. I'll have to stop flirting with Fintan. Never thought Fintan and I would make a good couple anyway. He's fierce handsome and quite charming but not flashy or spontaneous enough. Every Friday night after a long work week, I picture him heading to his favorite restaurant, where the host seats him at his regular table. He orders the same healthy dish and a red wine. No dessert, which is a shame since his black suits would certainly hide an extra stone."

I laughed. If I gained a stone—fourteen pounds—nothing would fit. "And his house is a lot of black-and-white, which also wouldn't suit you." However, the tree at his office was growing on me.

"Was nice of your handsome fella to repair my damaged painting." She peered over at the Charles Bridge artwork from Prague. "Looks like new. Was kind of you all to put everything back in order." She smiled. "You know the hero in all of this is Mac. To think I might never have confirmed my theory about Patricia Muir's biological father if he hadn't swallowed that emerald to later prove the jewel's authenticity. I have to meet the little fella sometime."

Mac didn't need to be trained to follow his instincts. Maybe he was merely a brilliant dog, not a bad one.

"You've gone above and beyond your job as an assistant. I hope this didn't scare you off."

Surprisingly, it hadn't. I shook my head. "I learned a lot."

"Actually, this was a new employee test, and you passed with flying colors." Winnie laughed. "Quite proud that my new protégé figured out the biological father mystery. You're going to make a brilliant genealogist."

A sense of pride brought a big smile to my face. "I knew

about the transfer of the hat between families. That was a huge clue in figuring out Patricia's parentage. The bigger question is, how'd you find Patricia Muir without the help of a DNA test?"

"The internet and Patricia's original birth record. I searched out her birth date online and had a hit. When she retired from teaching a few years ago, the school threw her a lovely going away party. There was a nice article in the local paper that included her birth date and that she was born in County Donegal but grew up north of Edinburgh. Eleanor would later end up in Donegal to teach and live with an aunt, who'd helped her through her pregnancy. Her aunt *Patricia,* who her daughter was named after. The fact that the adoptive parents kept the baby's given name at birth made me wonder if perhaps they were family relations. Curious about a connection between Aunt Patricia and the Muirs, I did a bit of research. It turned out the Muirs were related to Aunt Patricia's husband. So not a blood relation of the O'Sheas. At that point I was fairly confident that I had located Eleanor O'Shea's adopted daughter."

"Wow, that was some great detective work. Do you think that Eleanor knew who'd adopted her daughter or just asked her aunt to help find her loving parents?"

Winnie shrugged. "We'll never know. If she did know, she kept the secret even from her sister and best friend."

"Millie Moran wants Ella to keep a few jewels for her mother's health-care costs," I said. "The hat was intended to help women in need. Patricia Muir agreed. Oddly, if it hadn't been for Ella's aunt stalking Patricia, she might have died of a heart attack on her living room floor."

"Even though I opted not to press charges, the garda

aren't taking the break-in and destruction of property light-ly." Winnie shook her head. "How mad that the thief didn't turn out to be a rellie. I was certain it would be."

Or Mr. Buckley. Thankfully, I hadn't accused the man to his face, or it might have hurt our working relationship.

Despite being furious with his assistant and firing her, the lawyer had told the garda his house was in disarray after searching for misplaced keys. The garda didn't know the meticulous man well enough to argue the point. One less charge for Ella to worry about.

"I decided to pass on the Australia job. With everything going on, think I might be needing a bit more time to recover before making a long trip."

I nodded. "I agree."

"You may wish to know where one of my next jobs is before agreeing to it," Winnie said.

"Where?"

"The Hebrides, islands off the north coast of Scotland."

"Is that anywhere near Edinburgh?"

She shook her head.

I pictured Winnie and me kayaking between the islands, braving Scotland's brutal elements, Winnie's chunky stone necklace weighing her down so she didn't fly out of the kayak into the Atlantic while searching for a cemetery set high upon a cliff...

Wherever our genealogy research took us in the world, it was sure to be an adventure with Windiana Jones.

Eighteen

One Month Later

A warm breeze blew across the Daly estate's lawn, flirting with the chiffon sleeves of my cocktail-length white dress. I peered into my new husband's sparkling blue eyes as he slipped his arms around my waist and touched his lips softly against mine, sealing our vows. He drew back his head, smiling. I wiped traces of magenta-colored lipstick from his lips. The color matched his bow tie. Surprisingly, Mac had agreed to wear one. After all, he was one of the guys.

I glanced down at our ring bearer, who let out a happy bark, his first one since the ceremony had begun. I bent over and gave him a smooch, and Declan ruffled his furry head. Mac wriggled with excitement, swatting a playful paw at my magenta-colored headpiece. No gemstones or floral embellishments, the simple fascinator met Mac's approval. Zoe had found a winner!

Declan and his best man, Gerry, exchanged congratulations.

My sister, dressed in a magenta satin gown, wiped tears from her cheeks. "I'm so happy for you. And glad you didn't elope. This is one of our best days ever. I love you."

I smiled, giving her a hug. "Love you too."

Declan placed a warm kiss against the Claddagh ring on my finger. "I'll love you forever."

"About time you put a ring on it!" Zoe pumped a celebratory fist in the air. A fuchsia-colored hat with poufy feathers matched her dress, and her long blond hair was pulled back in a twist. She blew Declan and me a kiss, which we returned. She turned and shared a kiss with her boyfriend, Carrig.

The eighty-three guests stood, clapping. Gretchen queued the DJ to play "We Are Family" by Sister Sledge, keeping with the family tradition of the recessional song at George and Fanny's wedding. Gretchen stood in the back row with Nigel—dressed in a dapper black suit and bow tie, same as when we'd first met. They'd insisted on managing the wedding because Rachel wouldn't have trusted anyone else.

Neither would I.

Declan hugged his dad—a handsome man in his fifties, with graying hair, gentle blue eyes, and a charming smile. Exactly how I pictured Declan in twenty years, except Declan had bluer eyes, which he'd inherited from his mother. He embraced his mother, a short, trim woman who was going to make a lovely second mum.

"I'm so glad you made it," I told my dad. Thankfully, he was able to still walk after the long plane ride.

He smiled, beaming with pride like the time I'd caught a

huge bass when fishing at a cabin up north. "Wouldn't have missed it for the world. Looking forward to seeing your home in Ireland. Might just catch the travel bug like your mom."

Mom's eyes widened in surprise. "Are you saying you want to *get lost* with me?" She gave him a teasing smile.

"Not sure I'm up to an off-the-beaten-path tour quite yet," he said.

"Our home in Ireland is off a narrow road with sheep and tractors. The next best thing."

"Sounds perfect," he said.

George gave me a hug and then peered over at my mom. "Our mum is here with us and quite pleased that the Dalys and Coffeys are now getting on splendidly."

"She certainly is." Mom gave her brother a hug.

Their sisters, Dottie and Teri, went in for a group hug.

I thanked Thomas for trading in his yellow wellies and straw hat for a brown tweed blazer. He'd taken a break from his garden designing to attend my big day and to assist with our crazy upcoming wedding schedule. He also likely wanted to stand guard over his statuesque shrubs to make sure some crazed bride didn't slip a ballerina tutu on the *Venus de Milo*.

Grandma's niece and nephew, Sadie and Seamus, gave me enthusiastic waves. A fancy green hat with feathers sat atop Sadie's tightly curled gray hair. A dark suit swallowed the man's thin frame. Sadie's mother, Theresa, had written Grandma the letters I cherished, and she was in the photo on my dresser. George's aunt Emily, his father's sister and the former owner of our home, wore a bright smile despite being seated next to Cousin Enid. However, the older woman's usually rigid features were relaxed, and her gray eyes had a cheerful glint. I should probably stop referring to her as *nasty* Cousin Enid.

"*Something old, something new,* as the traditional saying goes," Winnie said. "For once at a wedding I'm not the *something old*." She chuckled. "But rather the *something new* as Caity embarks on a new genealogy career path." She smiled at Gretchen and Nigel. "Not that Caity won't still be helping out her old coworkers here occasionally, but ya won't be stealing her from me."

It appeared that I wasn't the only new addition to her life, but also Michael, whose teal tie matched his girlfriend's dress, proving he was flashy enough for my new boss's taste. The man was brimming with delight.

"I agree," Gretchen said. "Looking forward to new adventures."

"We'll have no shortage here, it appears." Nigel gave me a wink.

I'd come a long way over the past year. No longer a hot mess thanks to my professional and personal friends. My life was back on track. At least until Winnie and I ventured to the Hebrides in three days. Declan and I opted to put off our honeymoon and escape the dreary January weather to somewhere warm and sunny.

Declan and I finally reached the end of the aisle. He swept a steamy gaze down the length of my dress, mentally undressing me with a sexy little grin. "To think, a year ago I was zipping up the back of your sausage costume, and tonight I'll be unzipping your wedding gown."

I went warm all over, and my heart did a little jig.

The song ended, and I spontaneously tossed my bouquet into the air. Rachel caught Thomas's creation of purple and pink flowers. She snapped her head back in surprise, smiling at Gerry.

"We have availability at Christmas," Fanny yelled out.

"I just said I love you," Rachel said. "Not ready to say I do." She glanced over at Gerry. "Not quite yet anyway."

"At least he gave someone else a chance this time." Declan gave his buddy a pat on the back.

When Fanny tossed the bouquet at her wedding, it had flown past the women, toward Gerry's head. Shielding his face with his hands, he'd inadvertently caught the bridal bouquet. He was lucky a few of the single women hadn't fought him for it.

"Speaking of Rachel taking *baby* steps..." Mom slid me a curious glance.

"Time for a family photo," I yelled out to everyone.

The photographer gathered us up for a family portrait in front of the brick mansion. Declan and I stood in the center, Mac sitting obediently at our feet. Declan slipped an arm around my waist. I gazed into his blue eyes, a light flutter tickling my chest.

Standing on a ladder, the photographer tweaked our positions. "Almost perfect."

My life was beyond perfect.

"Stop!" a man yelled out.

A little late for someone to voice a reason why we shouldn't be married.

Everyone's attention turned to the older gentleman waving his hands wildly in the air, chasing after two sheep. The gatekeeper had been hired to prevent the rogue animals from accessing the estate during the wedding.

Mac shot from the group, racing toward the sprawling lawn of freshly mowed grass.

"Mac, stop!" Declan and I yelled in unison.

Our dog responded with several barks, continuing in hot pursuit of the trespassers. A few months ago, he'd found his calling as a sheep herder when Cousin Enid had intentionally let sheep loose on the estate.

"Hope he shut the gate after the sheep got in so Mac doesn't get *out*," Rachel said.

"No worries!" Gerry took off running toward the gate.

Thomas flew over to protect his shrubs.

"You did a brill job herding Carrig's sheep off the road and into the field at Christmas." Declan tugged off his black suit jacket.

I slipped off my white heels and tossed them to the side. "Let's do it!"

Declan and I took off after Mac.

Whether I traveled the world or remained at our lovely home to raise a family, life with Declan was sure to be an adventurous journey.

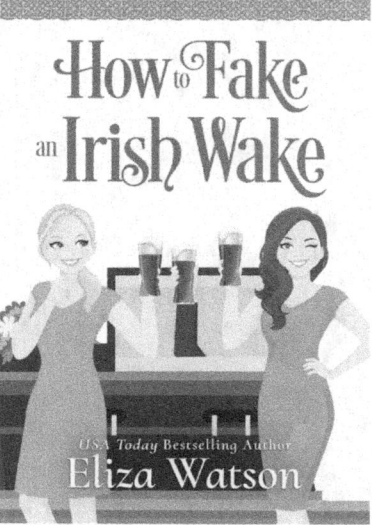

A Mags and Biddy Genealogy Mystery
Book One

Now Available

Author's Note

Thank you so much for reading *If at First You Don't Succeed, Fly Again.* If you enjoyed Caity's adventures, I would greatly appreciate you taking the time to leave a review. Reviews encourage potential readers to give my stories a try, and I would love to hear your thoughts. My monthly newsletter features genealogy research advice, my latest news, and frequent giveaways. You can subscribe at www.elizawatson.com.

Thanks a mil!

About Eliza Watson

When Eliza isn't traveling for her job as an event planner or tracing her ancestry roots through Ireland and Scotland, she is at home in Wisconsin working on her next novel. She enjoys bouncing ideas off her husband, Mark, and her cats, Frankie and Sammy.

Connect with Eliza Online
www.elizawatson.com
www.facebook.com/ElizaWatsonAuthor
www.instagram.com/elizawatsonauthor